LEGACY FROM SIRIUS

Borgo Press Books by JOHN RUSSELL FEARN

1,000-Year Voyage: A Science Fiction Novel
Anjani the Mighty: A Lost Race Novel (Anjani #2)
Black Maria, M.A.: A Classic Crime Novel
The Crimson Rambler: A Crime Novel
Don't Touch Me: A Crime Novel
Dynasty of the Small: Classic Science Fiction Stories
The Empty Coffins: A Mystery of Horror
The Fourth Door: A Mystery Novel
From Afar: A Science Fiction Mystery
Fugitive of Time: A Classic Science Fiction Novel
The G-Bomb: A Science Fiction Novel
The Gold of Akada: A Lost Race Novel (Anjani #1)
Here and Now: A Science Fiction Novel
Into the Unknown: A Science Fiction Tale
Last Conflict: Classic Science Fiction Stories
Legacy from Sirius: A Classic Science Fiction Novel
The Man from Hell: Classic Science Fiction Stories
The Man Who Was Not: A Crime Novel
One Way Out: A Crime Novel (with Philip Harbottle)
Pattern of Murder: A Classic Crime Novel
Reflected Glory: A Dr. Castle Classic Crime Novel
Robbery Without Violence: Two Science Fiction Crime Stories
Rule of the Brains: Classic Science Fiction Stories
Shattering Glass: A Crime Novel
The Silvered Cage: A Scientific Murder Mystery
Slaves of Ijax: A Science Fiction Novel
Something from Mercury: Classic Science Fiction Stories
The Space Warp: A Science Fiction Novel
The Time Trap: A Science Fiction Novel
Vision Sinister: A Scientific Detective Thriller
What Happened to Hammond? A Scientific Mystery
Within That Room!: A Classic Crime Novel

LEGACY FROM SIRIUS

A CLASSIC SCIENCE FICTION NOVEL

JOHN RUSSELL FEARN

Edited by Philip Harbottle

THE BORGO PRESS

MMXII

LEGACY FROM SIRIUS

FIRST EDITION

Published by Wildside Press LLC

www.wildsidebooks.com

DEDICATION

To the Memory of Ron Turner

CONTENTS

CHAPTER ONE 9

CHAPTER TWO 33

CHAPTER THREE 51

CHAPTER FOUR 71

CHAPTER FIVE 89

CHAPTER SIX 103

CHAPTER SEVEN 121

CHAPTER EIGHT 137

CHAPTER NINE 167

ABOUT THE AUTHOR 183

CHAPTER ONE

Robert Driscoll entered the sanctum of the President of the World Council with some nervousness. All the time he had been journeying by rocket-plane to this gigantic edifice, wherein was controlled the political and social destiny of the world, he had been wondering—wondering what on Earth could the President want with him? His position as Chief Observer for the New Mount Wilson Observatory gave him considerable standing, of course, but surely not enough to warrant a summons from the great man himself.

Bob Driscoll's speculations came to a stop when he finally arrived before President Alroyd's big desk. He stood looking upon a grey-haired, kindly man, beloved indeed by all the peoples of the world. Alroyd possessed the rare gift of being able to rule and still remain a human being.

"Have a seat, Mr. Driscoll," he invited, motioning. "I'm sorry I had to call you all the way from California, but it's most important. Indeed *vitally* important. I did not wish to entrust my information to television instructions for fear of something leaking out. That, you see, might have caused a panic."

Bob Driscoll did not see, even though he nodded profoundly. He took his seat and saw the President's grey hair haloed by the glow through the gigantic window. Outside, the spring sun was westering. In the distance, over a formidable barrier of soaring roofs a rocket-liner went down to its base.

"You will be aware," the President said, "as indeed everybody in the world must be by now, that we are enduring the most violent earthquakes in history. They keep on recurring without warning, and no scientists seem able to account for them—except to extend the rather nebulous theory that the Earth is becoming unstable and showing the first signs of breaking up."

Bob Driscoll nodded. "I've heard the reports, sir, even though I haven't experienced anything of that nature myself."

"The disasters are far-reaching." Alroyd rose to his feet, a tall, kingly man in sober regalia. "And we have got to get at the reason for them to see if something cannot be done to stop them, or at least forecast where they will happen next. That would give us time to save much life and valuable property. As it is, New York, London, Paris, Rio, and several other big cities have been shaken to the depths. Every day I receive fresh news of mounting death rolls, loss of property and priceless works of art...."

Bob Driscoll made no comment. Being still fairly young—thirty-four, to be exact—he would have preferred to come straight to the point. His good-looking face and keen blue eyes must have shown as much, for the President suddenly smiled and came round his big desk.

"We believe, Mr. Driscoll, that you and your fellow astronomers can help us," he explained. "Since an internal cause of the earthquakes cannot be detected, it seems logical to assume that the trouble might lie in the cosmos."

"In—what way, sir?" Bob asked, having the feeling that it was possible the President did not know what he was talking about.

"I, personally, am not an astronomer," Alroyd smiled. "But I have been informed by various scientific experts that the cause of our troubles might lie in something of the order of neutronium, densely heavy matter which in its passage through space is swinging all the planets in the solar system slightly out of balance by reason of its preponderant gravity."

"Yes, sir, I suppose that's feasible," Bob admitted. "It can be checked by the orbital movements of other planets."

"That is your sphere, Mr. Driscoll. What the Council wishes is for you to examine the problem with your fellow astronomers and then report your findings back to me. And remember!" The President raised a warning finger. "Not one word of this must go beyond the immediate scientific field it concerns. One hint that the world might be in danger would bring social and economic ruin down upon us."

"I understand perfectly, sir." Bob rose to his feet, sensing the interview was nearly closed. "The moment

I have an answer, I'll come personally to report it."

"Splendid! And thank you for coming."

Bob shook the hand of the ruler of the world and departed in something of a daze. He was troubled, too, more than he cared to admit. He had been hearing of the great earthquakes for several months now, and, like everybody else, had given them a good deal of thought, chiefly from the angle of a scientist. But he had never expected for a moment that he would be singled out as the man to explain them.

"Rather too much responsibility for my liking," he muttered, as he boarded the California-bound rocket-liner. "Don't know why I didn't take up a quiet life as a machine-hand or something instead of astronomy. If I don't provide a satisfactory answer to a command like this, I'm liable to lose my job, which in these days is not a pleasant thought."

All the way back to California from Washington he sat musing on the problem, hardly noticing the sky through which the liner hurtled, or the ever-changing pattern of the land below. He only got a grip on things again when the liner touched down at Los Angeles rocket-port. From here he took his own private helicopter to the heights of Mount Wilson where, on a massive and lonely peak, its top flattened by engineering genius, stood the greatest observatory in the world. It floated eternally above what few clouds there were in the Californian heavens. From it went forth all the world's astronomical information.

Bob hurried through the various clerical offices

until he came to the radio-room. Here he sat down and switched on the microphone connecting to speakers throughout the complicated building. Briefly he summed up his interview with the President, his words being transmitted not only to his own immediate staff but on private wavebands to every observatory throughout the world.

"So there it is, people," he concluded, cutting out the world-waveband and dealing only with his own staff—composed of twelve of the country's most expert cosmic-charters and astronomers. "Go to it. Get to the checking rooms and handle the reports as they come through. I'll go to work with 'Tiny'."

In various departments the men and women scattered, and Bob strode on his way to the observatory proper. He was thankful that so far the earthquakes had not shaken these remote heights of Mount Wilson, for the slightest disturbance might have thrown 'Tiny' right out of gear, and likewise thrown away some millions of American dollars.

As he walked over to 'Tiny's control-chair Bob felt once again that inescapable feeling and awe as he surveyed the giant—the world's greatest reflector, the utmost that the science and lensmen of this advanced age could produce. The 400-inch monster had an incredibly powerful magnification. Earth's nearest neighbour the moon—at an apparent distance of twelve miles—had been charted with absolute exactitude.

Bob seated himself, waiting for the roof dome to part in two hemispheres. Once this happened and the blaze of the night sky was above him, he began operating the mechanism. As he worked, he glanced now and again into the starry deeps—and smiled. Perched up here, wielding this giant, he felt like some superman peering into the beginning and end of the universe.

A faint click announced that the reflector was in position. Following out the cosmography he had learned so thoroughly, Bob started on his stellar check-up, giving his findings into the audiophone at his side. In turn this data was relayed to the checking rooms where the astronomical staff went to work with computers, spectro-checkers, and the other advanced appliances of their art.

"Neutronium!" Bob growled to himself presently, as he worked. "Wonder who in heck fed the President with that idea? Mmm—could be the solution, though, come to think of it, but if that were so the nearer planets would long since have developed bulges pulling out towards that excess gravity field."

'Tiny' swung silently on his mighty gimbals.

"Nothing doing," Bob muttered. "Mars, Venus, and even semi-plasmic old man Jove are all unchanged. Takes a bit of understanding! If these earthquakes are not caused internally *or* externally, what the devil is the explanation?"

He sat back from the controls wearily, pinching thumb and fingers to his eyes. His vision was strained with so much lens work and the study of display readings. Then as he sat there a sound caught his attention through the open dome—the thin, high scream of a descending rocket-plane. Somebody—and he knew whom—was heading for these heights of Olympus.

He waited, smiling in anticipation. He turned in the chair, his keen blue eyes lighting with pleasure as at last the observatory door opened and a slender figure in flying kit came hurrying across the waste of floor.

"Hello there, Bob!" The girl pulled off her helmet and shook free a mass of ash-blonde hair. "I thought I'd find you snooping around among the stars as usual. Beats me how you can stand the monotony!"

"I have to—or starve." Bob scrambled out of the control-chair and came forward to embrace the girl, then he held her a little away from him, studying her clear-cut sensitive features. It was rare indeed that he had the chance to see her. Her occupation as ace rocket-flier and leader of the Women's League of Rocketeers kept her fully occupied.

"Mona Driscoll," Bob said severely, all of a sudden, "I've a bone to pick with you! This Observatory is State property, and I've told you time and time again that the partners of employees are not allowed to...."

"Oh, skip it, Bob! Who'd crawl up six thousand feet of rock to check on your morals, anyway?" Mona gave her little ironical smile. "And anyway, you flatter your-self!" she continued. "I didn't come to gaze on your angelic face but to discover if you know anything about these earthquakes. Have you, perched up here like the Statue of Liberty, the remotest idea of what is going on below?"

Bob's lips tightened a trifle. He hedged.

"I've—heard, of course. Matter of fact, that's mainly the reason I'm here with 'Tiny'. I'm looking for a cosmic cause of the disturbances...."

"A *cosmic* cause? Good Lord, what do you expect to find way up among the stars to explain things? Sounds crazy to me—but then I'm only a woman with a smaller brain than a man."

Bob grinned. "Bird-brain or otherwise, darling, you still rate aces to me. As for finding explanations among the stars, I too, think it's haywire. But the high-ups have fed the President some kind of story about neutronium."

"Neutronium!" Mona gave her cynical smile. "My eye! If it were neutronium trouble we'd be having tremendous tides—and we haven't had; not any more than the quakes caused, anyway.... No," she continued seriously, "I think the trouble is deep in the Earth itself somewhere. From what I've seen of the ruins of Frisco, London, Paris, and other places, it looks as though the solution lies in internal explosions...."

"Without joking, you really think so?" Bob questioned.

"Uh-huh. Mind you, my geology has cobwebs on it, but I do think that if there were a way to study the roots of volcanoes we might get somewhere. Some volcanoes I've seen are blowing off hell whilst others are dead quiet for the first time in centuries. That seems to suggest a redistribution of underground pressure... or does it?"

"Maybe." Bob thought for a moment and then gave a

shrug. "Anyway, it makes no difference. You and I will keep on doing as we're told and stifle all natural urges to suggest something original—and by the way, what I've been telling you is a top-line secret. Not a word to anybody!"

Mona chuckled. "Great heavens, Bob, whoever heard of a woman talking?"

"Look, Mona, please be serious...!"

"All right, all right. I shan't tell a soul. You know me better than that, or should."

"Incidentally," Bob said, remembering something, "what were you doing in the danger spots like London, Paris, and so on?"

"Collecting important State documents—and occasionally people not so important—and flying them to places of safety. Supposed to be safe, anyway." She moved across to the control chair of the reflector, and lounged against it.

Bob stood thinking, hands in his pockets. "Mona, if these earthquakes go on...."

"We go out." She raised a shoulder. "The world will fold up like a conjuror's egg. Well—so what? We all die sometime. Just one of those things. Somehow, though, when you fly through the stratosphere at supersonic speed and get so close to the remoter deeps of space without actually touching them you don't feel afraid of dying. Neither should you, always gazing—up there!"

She turned and gazed at the twinkling diadem beyond 'Tiny's' mighty bulk. Bob gazed with her for a moment, caught in thrall by the immensity of space.

"I'm twenty-four now," Mona said, musing. "If I quit this mortal stage before I'm spreading myself out as a matron of sixty, it'll be all to the good. Think of my lines, beloved...."

She turned to meet Bob's serious eyes. Her smile faded.

"Just can't be serious, can you?" he asked, sighing. "For myself I think it's ghastly to think that we might be swallowed up by an inferno before we've even had the chance to find out much about each other."

"Maybe we'll die never knowing what we've missed," she reflected. Then she wrinkled her nose. "That sounds confoundedly morbid, come to think of it."

"Science ought to get busy!" Bob declared.

"Doing what?"

"We ought to have perfected and simplified space travel for one thing. Made it safer and easier—put it on a commercial basis, like we have with air travel."

"Supposing we had? The public would never take the risks. I know astronomers have a good idea of what dangers to expect on other worlds, but we don't know everything."

"We would with my projector as the white mouse," Bob said slowly.

"Projector?" Mona stared at him. "*What* projector? Don't tell me you've a magic lantern hidden away in that shack we call home."

"No, nothing like that. Just a theory I've got. Forget it. An idea I've doped out between times. Sometimes I have nothing to do up here but sit and think—and then I get the most marvellous notions."

"Maybe the altitude," Mona murmured, then turned and looked at the reflector. At the moment the tremendous mirror upon which it was focussed was blank.

"Any chance of one tiny little peep?" she asked coyly.

Bob sighed. "Oh, so you're after a star tour again, are you? One might think this reflector was installed purely for the spouses of astronomers to come and look through."

"Only one spouse, darling—or is there something I don't know about?"

"Stop clowning, can't you?" Bob roared; then he checked himself. "Okay—no harm in a little tour, I guess. The staff are busy at the moment checking on what they've got. Now, where'd you want to go?"

"Suppose you tell me? That'll give you a fine chance."

Bob gave her a look, so Mona relaxed and waited as the monster came to life again. Her eyes lighted with genuine pleasure. Bob stood beside her at the rail and together they gazed down on the mirror as the mammoth probe crawled at random through the firmament.

"There's something about this that always gets me," Mona whispered. "I don't know exactly what is it: perhaps the goddess in my wild soul."

"Peeping into eternity like this certainly does hit you in the eye," Bob acknowledged.

"Come to think of it, it would be rather wonderful if we could get safer and easier space travel. Be much better than strato-flying, anyway. That has so many limitations...."

Mona suddenly stopped talking—so suddenly indeed that Bob glanced at her in surprise.

"Anything wrong?" he enquired.

Mona did not answer. All recollection of what she had been saying seemed to have gone out of her head. She pointed to the reflector-mirror with a somewhat unsteady hand, pointed to a star which shone balefully bright. In the main it was blue-white, varying at times to an almost Martian red, then back once more to white.

"Bob, what star is that?"

All the habitual levity had gone from the girl's voice. It was strained; taut as steel wire.

"Why, Sirius," Bob answered, still astonished. "About the brightest star in the heavens. Star A in Canis Major, distance 8.7 light years...."

"It's horrible!" Mona whispered, and her face was drawn as she watched the star move through the graded squares on the mirror. "It's the most horrible thing I've ever seen!" she declared passionately.

Bob gave a rather uneasy laugh. "But that's absurd, Mona! It's really quite beautiful, especially now when one can sort of see it at such close quarters...."

He stopped, dumbfounded. Mona's legs had suddenly given way and she dropped soundlessly to the polished metal flooring. For about five seconds Bob just could not believe it. Mona, of the steel nerves, who was not afraid of dying, going out in a faint? Then he came to himself and lifted her limp body in his arms, depositing her in the control chair. Reaching out, he stopped the reflector mechanism.

"Mona," he said sharply. "Mona, what's wrong?"

For a while she lay sprawled in the snug grip of the chair; then, as he rubbed her hands vigorously, she began to show signs of recovery.

"Darling, what's wrong?" Bob caught her shoulders tightly and looked into her face as colour began to return to it.

She smiled wanly. "You're asking me! I—I— What on earth happened, anyway?"

"Why, you were talking about Sirius and then suddenly you went out like a blown flame." Bob grinned reassuringly. "Maybe it's the air up here. It does get you right in the middle sometimes. I've bowled over before today, especially with the dome open. Can't keep the air at normal pressure." He stopped and frowned. "But that should make your nose bleed," he mused. "And it isn't doing so."

"Maybe it would if you punched me on it for being such a fool."

There was silence for a moment, then Mona struggled unsteadily to her feet.

"No, it isn't the altitude," she decided. "I've been way up in the sky before today without an oxygen mask and my heart never missed a beat. First time in my life I ever did that. I just don't understand it! Maybe the old ticker's a bit overstrained from extreme acceleration. I've been doing a lot of fast rocket-flying lately."

Bob gripped her arm. "Better see a doctor, Mona. Promise me you will."

"You bet I will! I can't go risking other people's lives in a plane if I'm liable to go out like that...." Mona turned and gazed at the now blank mirror. "Almost looked as if something happened to me when I gazed at Sirius, didn't it? First time I've ever seen Sirius close up."

"Truly, but at other times we've viewed different parts of the heavens." Bob made a gesture. "Hang it all, dear, this is absurd. How could Sirius...?"

"Of course, how *could* it?" she exclaimed; then she smiled with something like her old carelessness and picked up her flying helmet from the table. "Just the same, Bob, I'm taking no more tours with 'Tiny' until I find out what's wrong with me. Maybe I've got astrophobia."

"Huh? What in blazes is that?"

"Fear of heights. Standing gazing into space on that mirror is a pretty dizzy business at that."

Bob nodded slowly, frowning. It struck him that Mona's conclusion was illogical. An ace strato-pilot bowling over just through looking into a space-mirror...?

"Well...." Mona tightened the helmet strap under her chin. "That seems to be all, except for goodbye. I've got to get back to the airport. No, no, don't worry about me!" she added quickly. "I'll be quite all right. See you at home—I hope."

She had been striding across the polished floor as she

spoke; now the door closed behind her. A few minutes later Bob heard her fast rocket-plane scream over the Observatory's lofty height. Through the big window he watched it descending in an 'S' of sparks towards the cloud-pack low down in the moonlight. Below, far below, lay Los Angeles.

Moodily, shaken by Mona's queer lapse, he turned back again to 'Tiny', switched it on again and studied Sirius for himself, long and earnestly. Certainly he could not see anything about it to occasion horror—nor did he feel unbalanced in any way. Finally he decided to study the data concerning the star.

"Spectrum deficient in dark lines, proving metallic absorption," he muttered. "Star not surrounded by metallic vapours, thereby putting it in Class B, totally apart from the G-type dwarf like our own Sun. A hydrogen envelope, mostly transparent...." He closed the file and scowled. "Damned if I know why I'm reading this stuff anyway!"

"Hello there!" the loudspeaker bawled suddenly, and Bob gave a start. He reached across and snapped on the microphone.

"Yes? What's wrong?"

It was the checking department. "Say, Bob, there's nothing here that shows any divergence. Better carry on with the eastern section. Whoever figured that neutronium might be out in space must have been nuts."

"I'm inclined to agree with you," Bob responded. "I'll carry on. Stand by for reports."

He switched off and with a troubled frown reseated

himself in the control chair and went to work.

* * * * * * *

Once she had arrived at the Los Angeles airport Mona went to the briefing room for her instructions, and found that they gave her about forty-five minutes breathing space before she had to take off for Rio. Just enough time in fact to see the airport surgeon.

As it happened he was on night duty, and greeted her in his usual matter-of-fact style as she walked into his office. He knew her well enough, since routine physical check-ups were the law for all men and women pilots engaged on public work.

"I think Bob may have been right, Mona," he commented, when she had outlined her disorder. "Probably the altitude. Anyway, I'll have a look. Step over here, will you?"

Gone were the days when a doctor had need to poke and probe. Mona simply stepped, fully clothed as she was, into a cabinet and the surgeon closed the door upon her. Beneath a battery of radiations, predominant amongst which were X-rays, every detail of her physique was reflected on to screens. Meters and gauges automatically showed respiration, heartbeats, and blood pressure.

Finally the surgeon switched off, unlocked the cabinet and Mona stepped out to find him considering his notes.

"I've seen a few healthy young women in my time, but few like you," he commented, smiling. "You check up in every detail, Mona—and with a heart like yours, you ought to live to be a hundred and fifty."

"You're not—just cheering me up, doc?" Mona asked, seriously.

"Why on earth should I? I state facts as I find them...." The surgeon put down his notebook and frowned at her. "What are you worrying about, girl? This machine does not lie, and it says you are in perfect health. Your fainting spell was purely the attenuated air of that Observatory; I'm sure of it."

"Yes—I suppose so." Mona reflected for a moment, and then she gave her sunny smile. "I've never been the worrying type, so I suppose I shouldn't start now. It's not the faint that has me worried, doc, but something else. The feeling of awful revulsion I had when I looked at Sirius in that reflector mirror. It was as though I'd looked at something indescribably obscene."

The surgeon shrugged. "Can't help you there, Mona. It's a mental reaction and a psychiatrist's job: I only deal with the body...."

He broke off, alert and listening. Mona, too, detected at the same moment a distant bass rolling sound. It only took her a second or two to interpret it—the same dreaded note she had heard in many a stricken city—

"Earthquake!" she gasped. "No doubt of it...."

She flung herself to the doorway with the doctor immediately behind her. The instant she reached the corridor the earthquake arrived in all its shattering fury. The rumbling became a roar, drumming above the steady crack of fissuring walls. Mona reeled and stumbled her way along the main corridor of the medical department, surrounded now by nurses and medical students who had also nothing in mind save escaping the disaster.

Panting for breath Mona reeled outside into the big open quadrangle of the building. Behind her, the big main edifice split and crumpled like grey tissue paper. Dazed she looked around her. The metal flooring of the quadrangle was splitting in all directions. In the distance buildings were visibly swinging out of the perpendicular and then avalanching downwards. Fire spurted reddishly in all directions; electric sparks flew as cables became entangled with metal. And the vast, overpowering din which gulped and rolled from the Earth's interior—

Then silence. So sudden it was startling. Steam hissed from somewhere. A chunk of metal dropped with a clang. Mona stood looking about her, disturbed air currents blowing a fast rising wind past her face. She began moving through the excitedly chattering medical staff, inwardly astonished at finding herself alive. Apparently the quake had been severe, but not of very long duration. Many light-standards were still standing, though some of them were drunkenly tilted.

She gained the main airport field to find that nothing was much disturbed. Her own rocket-flyer was just as she had left it.

"What's the damage, Harry?" she asked one of the ground mechanics.

"Pretty bad," Mrs. Driscoll," he answered grimly.

"Just had word through. Quake destroyed all eastern Los Angeles. We got the tail end of it."

Mona sighed as she climbed through the doorway of the flyer's control cabin.

"Bang goes our happy home," she commented. "It was in that part of the city. It's getting these days that you don't know where to settle."

"Sure is," the mechanic agreed, and slammed the cabin door.

At the same moment the door of the Mount Wilson Observatory opened, and Professor Leeman, curator of the observatory and astronomical figurehead throughout the world, came silently across the polished floor. Bob, at the end of his night's work on the reflector, turned in his control chair.

"Hello, Professor," he greeted respectfully. "I was just wrapping things up for the night."

Leeman nodded. He was a tall, gaunt, eagle-like being—forbidding in appearance yet good-natured enough upon close acquaintance.

"Feel the quake?" he asked brusquely, aiming sharp grey eyes.

"Slightly," Bob acknowledged. "Up here we have the mass of the mountain to support us. Just as well, too with so many valuable instruments about."

"Just so. I hear that all eastern Los Angeles has been smashed. Hundreds dead. Same old story."

Bob said nothing, his mind flashing instantly to Mona. He could only hope that she had been in the air when the quake had struck.

"I have here a report from the geologists," Leeman continued, taking a printed sheet from his inside pocket. "It makes hay of the idea that neutronium might be causing the earthquake trouble. Seismographers and geologists working together have positive evidence of an internal volcanic cause, so we can call the search for neutronium definitely off."

"I understand, sir," Bob assented. "And what about the President? Am I to tell him that?"

Leeman smiled frostily. "I have already done so. Naturally, it is no secret to any of us here that he gave you special orders. As chief curator my position ranks with yours."

Bob said nothing. If anything, the curator was a niche higher, but he never traded on his superiority.

"What we have to do," Leeman continued, "is follow out new Presidential orders. The geologists hold out little hope of stopping these quakes—so we have to prepare accordingly. The Space Agency have received orders to build Space Arks on the rocket-principle.... An ill-starred project, to my mind," Leeman finished gloomily. "However, the hand of urgency is pushing us. So, then, with your staff you will work out a full report on Mars—the only planet that we might hope to colonize. That clear?"

"Clear enough, sir," Bob agreed, reflecting. "Only I don't really see we have much to add to information already gained from the probes we sent to Mars years ago. Planets don't change much. Our trouble is, we don't have any probes there at the moment that are still transmitting. The government have scaled right back on expenditure on space exploration these last few years...."

"That's about to change," Leeman replied, with his usual brevity. "Anyway, those are the orders, Bob; I'm leaving it to you to carry them out."

With that he departed, leaving Bob looking thoughtfully after him. Fifteen minutes later Bob was leaving the Observatory for his State-maintained home two miles further along the mountain road. Actually, as Mona herself had remarked, it was little more than a large shack—but it served its purpose during long periods off duty. Besides, it gave him a place wherein to experiment.

He had only just risen from sleep the following afternoon when Mona came in, pulling off her flying kit wearily.

"Thank heaven you're still safe!" Bob greeted her. "I've had the wind up properly after that earthquake.... Did you see a doctor as you promised?"

"Uh-huh, and I think I must have been his last patient. I'm not sure whether or not he died in the earthquake. I only just escaped in time."

"Oh.... Well, what did he say?"

"Nothing the matter with me," Mona answered tiredly. "Nerves like cast iron, normal blood pressure, tough heart—I'm one hell of a woman in fact! But gosh, right now I'm worn out!" She sank down on the bed edge and looked at Bob with drowsy eyes. "I've been flying like a scalded hen ever since I left you last night—and talking of earthquakes, this is our home until we rebuild or everything drops to bits. Our suburb in Los Angeles collapsed last night and our ancestral pile with it. I flew across the region to make sure. So there it is."

"One home less to bother about," Bob growled, commencing to shave vigorously.

Mona was silent for a moment; then she asked:

"Anything fresh with you?"

"Not really—'cept that we're not looking for neutronium anymore. The geologists now believe an internal trouble is the cause of the quakes—same as you said. Our job at the Observatory is to find out everything we can about Mars, to which the high-ups are planning to evacuate some remnants of humanity. Tall order! You realize what it means, Mona? The Earth is considered doomed."

"Yes, I know." Mona's voice was listless. "The flying I've done recently has shown me that there are crackups everywhere. It's only a matter of time before these quakes bring civilization down round our ears...." A thought seemed to strike her. "Evacuation to Mars? When we haven't even set foot on the planet yet—except for robots!"

"The President doesn't give a thought to a trifle like that. The scientists and engineers will just have to devise something. Most people can think of something when their lives depend on it. What the World Council doesn't understand is that it takes time to develop a massive undertaking like that." Bob wiped his face decisively.

"To blazes with shop talk! You grab some sleep and I'll fix up a meal. Okay?"

CHAPTER TWO

When he returned to the bedroom-*cum*-living room, his culinary preparations complete, Bob found the girl sprawled out fast asleep. He moved around silently and settled down to eat, pulling a file from a nearby shelf, which he propped against the coffeepot.

"If one is to know sufficient about another world to be able to land on it in safety, mere spectroscopic analysis is not enough," he muttered. "Only way to get actual facts is to get real specimens from the planet concerned. And that, Robert, is where you walk in with a spatial projector. It could be done...."

"...there's danger there! Terrible danger! Be careful!"

Bob turned sharply as Mona made the observation. The question he had been intending died on his lips as he realized she was still sleeping, albeit uneasily, talking as she twisted about.

"Danger...Sirius!"

Sirius! Recalling the incident in the observatory, Bob got on his feet and went over to her. He listened tensely to her now scarcely audible mutterings.

"...You shouldn't have done it! You went too far! It means doom! Horrible doom! Why *did* you...?"

The sudden emphasis of her question awakened Mona. She looked about her in some bewilderment; then as she saw Bob's fixed gaze she started.

"Well, Rasputin, what's the matter with you?" she questioned.

"Eh? Oh, I...that is, you...."

"Mmm, coffee smells good," she exclaimed, stretching her arms. "I guess that sleep livened me up a little. See if I can't grab some more afterwards. Bob, what's wrong with you?" She contemplated him in surprise. "Why are you looking at me like that?"

"Just what is it about Sirius that means horrible doom?" he asked deliberately.

"Am I supposed to know?"

"Confound it, Mona, you were talking about it! In your sleep! I came over to listen to you."

"*I* was?" Her eyes widened. "*I* talked about Sirius?"

"That you did. And you talked about doom, too!"

Mona sat in silence for a while, her brows knitted. Then finally she gave a shrug.

"Be hanged if I remember a thing about it," she said. "Either you must be nuts, or else I am. Skip it anyway. Probably that queer turn I got last night, which is still repeating. I want a meal...."

She got up and went over to the table, seating herself. Bob's eyes followed her. Presently he came and sat down opposite her. She directed a curious glance towards the file propped against the coffeepot.

"What's this? A diary of your past?"

"No, the notes on my projector. I've been working

on it for ages at odd times. Now it may really be useful. Before a planet can be visited in safety it wants examining. A spaceship trip for tests would take too long and cost too much. With my idea that's all done away with. I can collect samples of air, minerals, and so on from any planet. Understand?"

"Certainly I do. A sort of—er—interplanetary garbage man."

"That isn't funny," Bob observed sourly. "My idea is to build a small automatic device which is a combined rock cutter, atmosphere sampler, tester, and so forth. In other words, a tiny automatic laboratory."

Mona nodded interestedly as she ate. The mischievous glint had gone from her eyes. Her virtue lay in knowing just when to cease being facetious.

"Assuming this box of mine were fired from here to Mars," Bob continued, "I would allow it about five minutes to reach that planet. Fifty million miles at the speed of light would be covered in approximately that time. The speed does the trick. Humans could not stand up to it, but a box full of mechanisms can. See? It would land on Mars quite safely and the automatic mechanisms would presently work. It would pick up the required samples, close itself, and be withdrawn to Earth. Radio and force beams would guide it there and back. Force beams to send it off; a magnetic beam to draw it back again. Guided by radio. Remote control on an interplanetary scale—and it could be done! Now laugh that one off."

Mona did no such thing. Her face, for some reason,

had become uncommonly grim.

"Well?" Bob asked at length. "Don't you see that once I've got a working model to show the scientists, which I can easily make here with the stuff I've collected, I could— Damnit, it might make my fortune! It would set us up beautifully if we have to become Martian colonists...."

"Bob, it's dangerous!" Mona interrupted him, putting down her sandwich. "I don't know why, but it is. Don't do it! Don't make this model!"

"What!" Bob stared at her blankly. "Now wait a minute! What about the danger if we stop here on Earth? What about the even greater danger of landing on a world that might kill us because of insufficient knowledge about it beforehand? What's the *matter* with you, Mona? First you talk in your sleep about Sirius and some kind of doom. Now you're even trying to tell me that my invention is a menace! *Why*?"

"I—I don't know. I wish I did."

"But you must! For heaven's sake be logical. Usually you are about the most practical girl on Earth."

"I know, but.... This is some kind of intuition." Mona rubbed her forehead vexedly. "Just a kind of feeling...."

She stopped in sudden alarm and gripped the table tightly as there came a bass rumbling from somewhere deep in the mountain range. It increased to a noisy growl and the floor began to sway distinctly back and forth for a moment or so. Then it ceased as abruptly as it had started.

Bob looked up at the swinging light cable.

"That must have been some quake to be felt right up here," he said grimly. "And it settles it for me, too! Danger or no danger, Mona, I'm going ahead. Can't be any worse than a ruined world, anyway."

Mona was silent, her expression moody. She went on with her meal without uttering another word. She had just finished it when the general radio speaker, always left in contact in these hectic days, came to life.

"Calling all emergency pilots! Calling emergency pilots! Return to Los Angeles base immediately and report for duty. Violent earthquake throughout entire Union. Special orders to be given."

"Which means me," Mona observed, making a wry face. She finished her coffee and then got to her feet. As she hurried into her flying kit she added, "Bob, please don't go on with this invention. I know it will bring disaster, though I can't explain how I know.... Please, promise me!"

"But I can't promise anything like that, Mona. It's too utterly unreasonable."

Her face became harder. "All right; but if anything happens—and it surely will—you'll wish you'd listened.... I'll be seeing you."

She headed for the door, then half way to it she paused and staggered a little, gripping the door frame for support. In an instant Bob had leapt to her side.

"Here, Mona, this won't do. In spite of what the doctor had to say, you're worn out...."

"No, no, I'm all right—really I am." Mona straightened up and breathed a little more rapidly. "Just another dizzy spell got me...." She hesitated, frowning. "I—I saw something for a moment," she continued in wonder.

"Huh? What exactly?"

"It's absurd, of course, but it was momentarily bright, like a flashing picture. I—I saw some kind of machinery. And Sirius! No mistake about that! Only it was a yellow Sirius instead of blue-white."

"You're perfectly sure it was Sirius?" Bob insisted.

"I'd swear it on a stack of Bibles if need be...," Mona broke off. "What in heck am I talking about anyway? Either I'm going crazy or else old age is coming on. You puzzle it out, Bob; I certainly can't. I've work to do."

She was gone before he could question her further. From the doorway he watched her climb into the rocket-plane. He waved as she took off, then returned pensively into the shack.

"Yellow, not white," he mused. "Hmm! In the life-table of the giant stars like Sirius that could mean when it was much younger. Orange, yellow, white, blue-white—countless ages ago it would have been yellow."

By this time he was fully conscious of the deep mystery of the problem. Mona was not ill: even without the doctor's assurance he could feel sanguine about that. Her spirits were too high, her sense of fun too keen. But there was something else the matter—something apart. And back of it, utterly unexplained, was Sirius.

"Oh, damned if I know!" he snorted at last. "Maybe

she's right in saying one or other of us is nuts."

He swung aside impatiently to the little room he used for his workshop, took his file of notes with him, and studied it carefully before making preparations. But as he worked, he kept on wondering. The warning Mona had given him remained embedded in his mind and just would not be shaken free.

* * * * * * *

Desperate events being enacted far below the clouds at the lower levels of Mount Wilson kept Mona away from the shack for some days afterwards, during which time she was forced to be constantly on the move. She knew perfectly well that she went with her life in her hands on every trip she made. Normal flying laws had gone by the board. The climate, even in the calm Californian region, was utterly crazy in every part of the world. She rode tempests side by side with thousands of miles of calm sun or moonlight. Below her she had a patchwork vision of mighty cities laid in ruin, of drifting hordes of people forced to be. nomadic by reason of the grim danger which beset them. Probably not since the Glacial Epoch had there been such a wholesale movement of people, all of them falling back upon the herd instinct in their common predicament.

At times Bob heard from Mona over the radio. Indeed it was through her that he realized the full extent of the disastrous earthquakes convulsing the world. Not that he had much time to consider the matter. He was kept constantly busy in the Observatory, trying to discover from past and present records what lay ahead for possible Martian colonists,

Bit by bit, at favourable times, he wedged in hints about his invention—and at last succeeded in getting the matter-of-fact Professor Leeman interested.

"If you've really got something as good as you describe it, Bob, then go right ahead with it," Leeman said. "As you say, we cannot be too sure of the planet we intend to visit. If things come to a head, we'll need all the beforehand data on Mars we can get. Yes, go on with this model, and if it's okay, I'll fix the right men to see a demonstration."

"It's mainly a matter of time, sir," Bob explained hesitantly. "I mean, I'm here all night, grab a bit of sleep by day when I can, and...."

"You're released from duty here until you get your model finished," Leeman decided. "The staff can carry on. I'll arrange it. You seem to have something really important, so give all your time to it and advise me when you're ready."

"Thanks, sir. I'll do just that."

Bob took him at his word and departed forthwith. Thereafter he spent every waking hour at his model, eating irregularly, talking to Mona at times on the radio. His only awareness of the outer world danger was an occasional violent trembling of the shack, which passed as rapidly as it commenced.

At the end of a week of brain and body flogging, he had the model finished, had even made two complete systems of minute remote control—force and magnetism.

"What more do you want?" he breathed, rubbing his hands. "In exactly one hour I shall be demonstrating at the Observatory! And will it make their eyes pop!"

He felt rather Faustian standing here under the single light in the workshop, whilst outside a violent storm had risen—the first storm he had ever known in these clear, rarefied heights.

Cascades of rain were battering against the windows, hurled by a screaming ninety-mile-an-hour gale. Not that the storm surprised him. He had been wondering how long it would be before the atmosphere up here started reacting to the discharged gases from the earth-quake chasms.

"Hello there!" called the emergency radio speaker. "Hello! Mona Driscoll aboard Z-60 calling...."

Bob reached out and closed the switch. Mona's voice had been distorted with violent static.

"Come in, Mona," he intoned. "Over to you."

"Switch on the landing light, will you Bob? I'm flying blind in this soup."

"You're crazy to even try landing on a mountain side in this!" Bob yelped.

"I'd be crazier still to be trying to fly in it. I'm coming in. Switch on the lights and stop preaching!"

Bob knifed in the switch that actuated the single, guiding searchlight outside; then he listened anxiously for, and presently heard, the splutter of rocket-exhaust tubes above the din of the hurricane. As he opened the shack door Mona came hurrying in, her leather flying togs black and sodden with rain.

"Nice weather we're having," Bob commented, heaving against the door to close it. "Come to California and bask in the golden sunshine!"

"You should get an eyeful of it down below!" Mona told him. "Whew, I never saw anything like it! Full blown hurricane which makes a Florida whirlwind seem like a zephyr."

She threw herself in a chair and rested for a moment. Then she continued, "I've been tearing about everywhere these last few days, sleeping and eating how and where I could. The whole continent's cracking up, Bob, like a rotten accordion. According to the radio, it's pretty much the same the world over...."

"You had your nerve risking this storm on the mountain heights. Here, come and get those wet things off...."

"No time," she interrupted. "In any case, these togs are waterproof. I had to come along personally to get these"—and rising, she took a bottle of restorative pills from the cupboard—"and to tell you about my next assignment. You won't like the sound of it."

"I don't like the sound of you dashing about anyway. Where this time?"

"I'm leaving right now for Buenos Aires."

Bob stared. "What! In *this*? Why, it's close on six thousand miles...."

"I know, but it's got to be done." Mona took one of the pills. "You see, so far Buenos Aires has escaped the worst, and I have to fly a plane full of important secret Government papers there right away, storm or no storm."

"It's suicide!" Bob declared angrily. "What the devil do these fools of airport authorities take you for?"

"What I am—a public servant." Mona sighed and glanced at the window as the rain battered furiously against it. "I'll make it," she decided quietly. "But Bob, it's just in case I don't that I...wanted to see you again. I hope that doesn't sound too mushy, but you're not a bad husband at that."

Bob caught her in his arms for a moment. "Mona, I do wish you didn't have to do this," he entreated. "I know you've got courage—too much, maybe. That's why they load the toughest assignments on to you. I'm sure you can never make the trip in this!"

"I'm afraid I've got to." Her blue eyes were perfectly steady. "It's my task, just as much as the Observatory is yours Talking of that, how are you getting on? I couldn't tell very much from the radio. Static warped it."

"Oh, I'm getting along fine. As I told you over the radio, I've been released from Observatory work so I can get on with my projector. I've finished it. In less than an hour I have to demonstrate...."

"You *finished it*? In spite of my warning?" Mona's voice had become suddenly sharp.

"Yes, in spite of your warning. Come and take a look for yourself and see how wrong you were." Bob preceded her into the workshop and as she came up behind him he motioned to the apparatus.

"There it is! Once we get the thing made on a big

scale, we can get all the stuff we need from other worlds and so be sure of what we...."

"Bob, I gave you a solemn warning," Mona broke in on him. "You ignored that warning—therefore, for your own sake—for everybody's sake in fact—I've got to act. Nobody must ever see this thing. Nobody! Understand?"

Bob wheeled round on her, staring incredulously.

"No, I certainly don't understand!" he retorted. "I was released from duty specially to get this thing done. If I don't produce the goods, I'll lose my job. Good heavens, Mona, I'll look like a kid whose played hooky. What you have got to realize is that I...."

"Realize nothing!" Mona shouted, flushing.

She looked about her quickly, then before Bob could focus on her intentions she whipped up the heavy chair from beside the bench, whirled it over her head and slammed it clean into the midst of the delicate equipment. It crumpled instantly, wires and components scattering about the floor.

"There!" Mona flung the chair back into position. "I did that for your own good...."

Swept with sudden fury Bob swung on her and tried to seize her—but she twisted away. Her expression had an odd mixture of sorrow and anger. There were tears glinting in her blue eyes.

"Please try and understand, Bob," she implored hoarsely. "I had to do it!"

"You idiot!" he raved. "You damned little fool! Do you realize what you've done...?"

Control transiently deserted him. His palm came round and struck her sharply across the cheek. For a moment she staggered, and then straightened up again, biting her underlip.

"Mona, I didn't mean...." Bob stopped, utterly appalled by his action.

"Oh, I don't blame you," she said quietly. "Maybe you'll realize some day what I'm driving at. Maybe even *I* will, too. I certainly don't so far."

She swung and headed for the outer door, strapping her helmet in position. Bob raced after her and caught her arm. She pulled free impatiently, however, and marched out into the screaming wind and deluge of rain.

In the doorway Bob halted, waiting, glumly watching the dimly-lighted rocket-plane as it lifted with difficulty into the hurricane. Slowly he turned back into the shack and wandered once more into the workshop.

At about the same moment Mona settled herself more comfortably at the control panel of her little flyer. Back of her, in the dark rear of the vessel, were the heavy metal cases which contained the Government papers and securities. Somehow, no matter how frightful the journey, she had got to land them at Buenos Aires airport, and there her responsibility would end.

Moodily, her actions back in the shack still clouding her mind, she set her course by the instruments, steadily gaining altitude in an effort to rise above the storm. Not that she was particularly successful. For every hundred feet the rocket-plane gained it fell back thirty, tossed and twisted around helplessly by the hurricane blasts screaming out of the dark.

Intent on her instruments, her only means of feeling her way through the chaos, Mona had little interest in the rain streaming down the outlook window. Nor was she alarmed by the fact that she was alone in this little world of hers, hemmed in by a violent storm, her only chance of survival the delicate scientific equipment struggling to show her the course.

As near as possible she was trying to follow a straight line, which, once she had crossed Southern California, would take her across the lonely Pacific Ocean until she touched South America at Antofagasta. The rocket-plane had fuel and to spare for the trip; she herself was prepared to keep alive and awake by restorative pills. The only thing that could stop her was the tempest.

Steadily she still fought for altitude, the view outside—such as it was—lighted ever and again by a savage fork of lightning. It turned the rain-swamped ports into scintillating rectangles for a second, giving beyond them a vision of smoky, heavy clouds boiling in the terrific wind pressure. The machine swayed beneath her as if she were on the ocean—but still she went on resolutely...until, quite unexpectedly, she sailed above the storm region into quiet moonlight.

"That's better," she muttered, with a sigh of relief, and gazed upon the glittering stars and, far below, the scudding of the storm clouds, flickering with the lightning discharging through them.

She put on speed, climbing the acceleration until

she was hurtling through the moonlit night at eight hundred miles an hour, the rocket-tubes delivering a steady throb of power. Her instruments told her she was over the Pacific Ocean, but of the water itself she could see no trace. Everything down there was blanketed in the storm.

Relaxing, her fingers light upon the controls, she gave up her mind to other matters. Her strange intuition, which had caused her to destroy Bob's valuable model. It was something she just could not understand; something indeed for which she hated herself bitterly. She loved Bob dearly, and the last thing she would ever have normally done would be to destroy a work on which he had laboured so long. The train of her thoughts brought her to looking at Sirius—glowing, baleful, amongst the hosts of heaven. Baffled, she stared at him, yet felt none of those strange sensations she had encountered when viewing him through the reflector-mirror at the Observatory.

One hour crawled into two—into three—and then four. She was still screaming her machine like a bullet at the undermost limit of the stratosphere. Shortly it would be dawn. She yawned and wriggled stiffly. Below there were still storm clouds rolling ominously—too ominously. The further onwards she flew the higher the disturbances seemed to get. It was when she was within two hundred miles of Antofagasta, the westernmost point of South America as far as she was concerned, that she realized she would have to do battle with the storms again. They were evidently spreading into the upper reaches of the atmosphere.

Watching through fatigued eyes she saw the clouds mounting up ahead of her against the dimming grey of the sky, for the dawn was not far away. They loomed as a curtain drawn across the paling stars. Then she had plunged into it and it seemed as if the hurtling rocket-plane had been struck by a vast hammer.

She had been prepared for a violent atmospheric bumping, but hardly anything like this. Lightning blazed at her with bewildering nearness, sending ripples of electricity up and down the port's outer frames. The sense of static tension made her feet and fingers tingle. If there were thunder, she could not hear it. The roaring of the wind and the coughing splutter of the rocket-motors made it impossible for anything else to be detected.

With every trick she knew she tried to gain height—and failed. It was no fault of the machine. It was simply that heavier air above was pressing downwards with the force of countless tons, battering the machine down from the heights, deeper and deeper into the area of seemingly endless storm.

Alarm began to seize Mona for the first time. The instruments, affected by the lightning, had gone haywire and no longer gave her a true course. To the best of her knowledge from the hasty calculations she made, she was being swung northwards, driven by the hurricane in a north-eastward direction. Hence, unless a caprice of the wind altered things again she must presently cross Bolivia, and after that drive straight across the still uncharted wastes of Brazil.

She remained in the control chair, anxious to snatch the merest glimpse of what was transpiring outside, but as time passed she gave it up. The machine was out of control, her eyes were aching from the endless intermittent flashes of savage lightning. Then she caught sight of the altitude-gauge. She was flying now at little more than 5,000 feet and dropping lower with every movement. This in itself seemed to her a fatal happening. From her earlier flying experiences in the territory, in favourable weather, she knew that somewhere ahead lay the Sajama Mountains, reaching to a full 20,000 feet. If in the grip of the storm the flyer were hurled into there, nothing could save her.

The thought of death did not particularly alarm her; she had known ever since being a strato-pilot that she might have to face it one day What *did* grieve her was that she had left Bob on the oddest note since their marriage. Just a few words might at least straighten things out and leave her memory a little less bitter.

She reached out to the radio equipment, though she had little hope of transmitting an understandable message amidst such static. Before her hand could contact the switch, however, a downrushing blast of wind struck the flyer with shattering impact The vessel twisted round crazily, flinging Mona out of the control chair. Through the port window amidst the incessant flashing of the lightning she had a vision of wildly gyrating tree tops. Then it seemed as though a wilderness of branches was hurtling straight for her.

The window splintered but did not break. The machine slewed crazily round, flinging Mona to the far end of the control room. She lay gasping, hanging desperately to a stanchion, convinced the machine was crashing to its final destruction somewhere in the Brazilian forests.

CHAPTER THREE

Through the wild night Bob did what he could to patch up the model which Mona had so ruthlessly smashed. In between times he answered the Observatory phone, each time stalling the impatient enquiries of Professor Leeman as to how much longer he was going to be.

Finally, however, it seemed that Leeman's tolerance was at an end. Bob answered a thunderous hammering on the shack door to find the curator, protected by transparent slicker against the fury of the rain, standing outside.

"What the devil's the meaning of this, Bob?" he demanded, striding in amidst a flurry of raindrops. "Do you realize that the Governors, myself included, have been kept waiting five hours? I don't mind so much for myself because I know it takes time to make a model—but I can't hold them much longer. You said you'd be ready around midnight."

"Uh-huh," Bob agreed moodily, when he had shut the door.

Leeman looked at him keenly from under his dripping helmet.

"As it happens the storm has kept the Governors in the Observatory, otherwise they'd have gone long ago—what's gone wrong?"

"I—I had an accident with the model, sir," Bob lied, motioning to it. "As I told you over the phone. Take a look at it for yourself."

Leeman moved to the bench and considered the half completed apparatus with its dented sides; then his gaze moved on to the dozens of components still to be fitted into place.

"Accident, or temper?" he asked curtly, turning.

"How do you mean?" Bob questioned, conscious of an inner sullen anger.

"This doesn't look like an accident to me, Bob. From the dents and damage I'd say you smashed this whole thing on the floor or something, probably because you'd become impatient with it. I've done that myself before today."

Bob met the cold, sharp eyes and came to the conclusion that he was doing himself no good by taking the blame. "My wife is the cause of everything," he said bitterly. "It was she who smashed it, just before she left here for Buenos Aires. I'm afraid I—I hit her across the face in my fury.'"

There was a silence for a moment, save for the din of the storm outside. Then Leeman gave a shrug.

"I'm afraid domestic issues have nothing to do with it, Bob. I don't even know if I believe you. Mona has never struck me as being the kind of girl to damage your reputation—for that has most certainly happened now. You realize what will happen?"

Bob was silent.

"I shall have to explain to the Governors that you have not got the model finished. After my summoning them specially to see it, they'll have only one reaction—to discharge you. You were granted special time to get the model finished, and it will seem to them as though you have just wasted your efforts.... Do you think you can piece this thing together if you go on working at it?"

"No," Bob answered grimly. "It's knocked about too much. I can build a new model, but that may take several weeks."

"Which won't do at all." Leeman gave a shrug. "Well, there it is, Bob. I'll do what I can to soften things, but I don't hold out much hope."

With a rustle of waterproofs, he strode to the door and dragged it shut behind him. Bob remained exactly where he was, staring fixedly at the scattered components and dented plates.

"Why?" he breathed, bewildered. "For Pete's sake, *why*? What possible harm can there be in making a machine like this? The only possible way of being sure what any planet contains. Sirius," he went on, brooding. "There is the mainspring of the whole business. Sirius, as the star probably was some thousands of years ago. Yellow, not white—some throwback to ancient history?"

He frowned over this, his interest in the problem by far outweighing the thought of discharge. Turning to his assortment of astronomical books, he began to browse thoroughly through them; but finally he arrived at the conclusion that he knew more on his own account from Observatory surveys.

"Of course," he commented, to the empty air, "Sirius transmits radiation more freely than other stars, since his envelope consists almost entirely of hydrogen. He transmits light-waves with intense power, hence his brilliancy. He *could* transmit other waves in like proportion...."

"Hello, hello! Mona Driscoll, Z-60, calling!"

Bob sprang to his feet in joyful surprise and closed the main radio switch that activated the microphone.

"Mona, am I glad to hear you!" he cried. "Look here, I've been doing a lot of thinking and I want to apologise. I'm sure you weren't personally responsible from what you did to my projector— Over to you," he broke off, as the emergency light flashed desperately for him to shut up and listen instead.

"Keep your apologies," came Mona's voice, blurred and unreal with atmospherics. "You wouldn't have been human if you hadn't blown up after what I did— Listen, I'm stranded! I've tried contacting other stations and plane depots, but most of 'em are either too busy or too cold in the feet to bother over me. I've come down somewhere in Brazil, the plane's folded up around me, and the miracle is that this radio still works.'"

Bob stared at the radio-speaker. As a background to Mona's voice there was swishing rain and moaning wind, and that ever present blurring static.

"Whereabouts in Brazil?" he questioned.

"Lord knows! I was heading okay for Antofagasta, then I got caught up in a storm belt and flung north-eastwards. I'm on the edge of some kind of forest region. The real forest, at a rough guess, is some fifty miles further on. I seem to have come down in a valley. It's a queer sort of valley, too."

"Why queer?" Bob asked, as she paused.

"Well, unless my eyes are playing tricks—which wouldn't surprise me after the lightning I've been through—this valley is full of statues. My searchlight's still working and I can see 'em plainly."

"Statues?" Bob repeated blankly. "Sure you haven't been dreaming?"

"I'd like the chance to. I'm fagged out. How about some help? I don't see why you should sit all warm and cosy whilst I catch pneumonia. Or don't I rate anything after the way I behaved?"

"You're my wife, and I've already said I forgive you," Bob growled. "Sure, I'll come and find you. Matter of fact, if you hadn't bust my projector—and incidentally got me the sack!—I'd probably have been at the Observatory now and missed your message."

"Did you say 'sacked'? I never...."

"All right, Mona, skip it. We can talk later. I'll start off right away and you can guide me by radio."

Bob switched off and scrambled over to his pilot's rig, hastily clambering into it. Once he had plunged into the night it took him fifteen minutes of battling with wind and rain before he got to the Observatory hangars. Nobody was around as he took off in his private plane. Presumably the Governors were still debating his fate, unless the storm settled it for him anyway.

As it had been for Mona, so it was for him—blind flying through the tempest with the raging scum of cloud all around him. At intervals Mona's voice came through the radio, and her comments became increasingly surprising to Bob as he manoeuvred and twisted the rocket-plane on its course, buffeting right and left.

"...valley of statues is right," came her voice. "It seems to me as though the stone lying around here isn't natural stone. It's got a queer, flaky look. In fact I wouldn't be surprised if the valley itself was not in view at all until the earthquakes played havoc with the topography. Wonder who'd put statues around here, anyway? You still alive, Bob?"

"Yeah," he acknowledged briefly. "Check the course."

She did so and then continued, "Yes, I'm sure this place was formerly buried under a sheet of stone which cracked wide open. Somehow it looks—kind of *familiar*."

"Familiar? And when did you ever tour the wilds of South America?"

"Never, of course. I've only flown over this region. But I've a sort of recollection that I've seen it all before somewhere. Silly, isn't it?"

"No more silly than when you looked at Sirius through the reflector-mirror and passed out."

"Um...Sirius. Maybe that links up somehow, too."

This speculation seemed to preoccupy Mona, for she only spoke thereafter to give the course. Until at last after seeming ages of zigzag flying through the blinding, flashing storm Bob began to feel his way downwards through the rolling clouds With difficulty he made a landing on the stony valley floor, then climbed out of the machine into a shrieking gale as the girl came running up in the blaze from her wrecked plane's searchlight.

"Nice work," she shouted, adding naively, "Maybe you should have been a strato-pilot instead of an astronomer."

"Never mind the cracks!" he bawled. "Let's get clear of here whilst my plane's still in one piece. Hop in...."

"No, no, I can't do that. There's work to be done first. I've valuable papers to shift. Come on; you'd better give me a hand."

Battling with the wind they returned to what was left of her plane.

"You're right, there sure are plenty of statues around here," Bob yelled, as Mona loaded his arms with tin boxes and mackintosh-covered wads of deeds. He looked about him in the immediate area of the searchlight. Within the space encompassed by the glare there were a dozen or so stone figures in all manner of postures, most of them lying flat on the cracked stony ground.

"Perhaps some ancient form of Madam Tussaud's," Mona said. "Okay, that's one load. I'll collect some more whilst you dump them in your plane. The most important ones are here, so watch yourself."

Bob had hardly arrived back at his machine and rid himself of the documents before he detected an ominous sound above the scream of the storm. There was a low, growling rumble, which increased rapidly to a tearing and rending.

He lurched forward, staggering helplessly on to his knees as the ground jerked to and fro beneath him. A noise like a thunderclap bit into his ears. Desperately he jerked his head round and was just in time to see the statue-covered floor split in twain between himself and Mona.

A section crumbled inwards, gulping down the girl herself, her plane, and crumbling stone besides. Then as suddenly as it had commenced the quake ceased.

"Mona!" Bob yelled hoarsely, scrambling to his feet. "Where are you? *Mona...!*"

He went staggering across to the gap and stared into it. There were no sounds from within it—nothing indeed except the howl of the storm. For just a moment panic touched him; then he mastered himself and raced back to his plane for an electric torch. Returning with it he flashed the beam urgently into the hole.

As he did so, there belched forth more rumbling and growling, deep down in the earth somewhere. He ignored them and kneeled, gazing down at a crumpled mass of plane wreckage some thirty feet below. There was also the dimly visible white spot of the girl's face. Her water-soddened flying kit gave back no reflection at all.

His survey took no more than a matter of seconds, then he lowered himself over the edge of the hole and fished in the darkness below. He found a foothold with difficulty and began to slide, clinging to stonework as he went. He had got halfway down the slope when the still rumbling earth gulped again and wrenched free his grip. He crashed the remaining distance and landed on his back with teeth-jarring impact. On top of him came a deluge of small stones—then the din of the storm above suddenly ceased.

Aching, fingering his bruises, he got up and felt around for his torch. Finally he encountered it and switched it on. His lips compressed at what he beheld. The gap through which he had climbed had closed itself up! The two sides of the top had fallen together and interlocked themselves.

"Never thought I'd crawl into my own grave," he muttered; then he scrambled to Mona's side as she lay motionless beside the wrecked plane. Catching her shoulders he shook and slapped her into consciousness. She began to stir uneasily and finally looked about her.

"What the...?" She tenderly rubbed a bruise on the back of her head. "Ouch, that's a tough one!" she muttered. "What hit me? Where are we, anyway?"

"Buried alive, near as I can figure it."

Mona gazed at Bob's worried face in the torchlight. "Buried alive? That's a pleasant notion...."

"The earthquake started the job; then just as I'd got below here there was another tremor—which finished things." Bob directed the torch beam up to the roof. "Look for yourself. The gap I came through is sealed up solid."

Mona looked, but the thought of being entombed was so terrifying a one that it did not register immediately.

"How are you feeling?" Bob asked her.

"Oh, I'll be all right, I guess." She got on her feet rockily, Bob holding her arm. She was still looking at the roof. "Well this is a nice, cheerful outlook anyway!" she complained. "The plane's pretty badly smashed up, too—worse than it was before. Radio's shot to blazes, so I don't see us doing much communicating with the outer world."

"We may as well face it," Bob said quietly. "Unless a miracle happens, we're going to pass our last hours down here. It's impossible to smash a way through all that stone above. In fact, we'd probably bury ourselves under the stuff even if we tried."

"Sounds defeatist to me," Mona decided. "I'm not giving up that easily. What else is there?"

Bob flashed the torch around again—then his eyes narrowed in sudden hope as he beheld a jagged fissure in the far wall of this little 'grave'.

"May be worth looking at," he said as Mona followed his gaze.

They moved over to it. Very carefully Bob eased his head through the crack, pushing the torch through at a level with his waistline. He could hear Mona's voice dimly.

"I'll bet you never had such fun since you got your neck stuck in the bed-rails! Mind that gap doesn't close up suddenly!"

Bob withdrew his head after a while ,and dragged out the torch. Its beam cast into his incredulous features.

"Now what?" Mona asked in surprise. "Have we landed on a South American gold mine or something? Be just about our luck when we can't get out and spend the money!"

"No, no, not gold," Bob said quickly. "There's statues by the million beyond this wall—well, dozens of 'em, anyway," he amended. "And there's also some kind of machinery modelled in stone. Go on—take a look for yourself."

"Uh-huh, I think I'd better."

Mona took the torch and inserted her head through the narrow gap. Long and earnestly she gazed into a vast underground hall that had the earthy, mouldy smell of long burial.

As far as the torch beam could reach were statues and, as Bob had said, the ghostly outlines of machinery.

"Right enough," she assented, drawing herself free again.

"But what in the world are we supposed to make of it? Who'd want to do sculpture down here, anyway?"

"I dunno—but we're going to try and find out! There may be a way to the exterior through that hall. Seems to me as though we've stumbled on an ancient crypt, city, catacombs, or something—South America's a happy hunting ground for them, anyway. Here, grab this chunk of rock and hammer away with me. Maybe we can make this gap wide enough to permit us scrambling through."

Bob put down his torch so that the beam illuminated the crack; then he and Mona set to work together, banging with all their strength. The queer flaky rock chipped gradually under the onslaught—but it was two hours and more before they had made enough space to allow their bodies to squeeze through the space.

"I'll go first," Bob said finally, and taking the torch he just managed to slide through the fissure. For Mona, with her slender build, it was an easier task. Silently they stood surveying the mystery in the torchlight.

"This is no more than we saw when first we looked," Mona said. "Let's take a closer look."

They began walking in wondering silence through the cavernous immensity, ankle-deep grey dust stirring around them in a fine haze.

"This place must extend for the devil of a distance," Bob commented at length. "Even the torch beam doesn't anywhere near penetrate to the end of the vista...."

He came to a halt and scratched his head, staring around at the stone-sculptured machinery rising in places to the lofty roof.

"I guess this roof must go up to form the side of the valley." he continued. "This machinery here is complete to the last detail, too. Look at this.... Even these tiny threads of wire are faultlessly modelled in stone."

"Somehow it reminds me of a ship caked in ice,"

Mona said striking an apt simile; then she too, paused in her wanderings and gazed at a surprising pair of statues.

There was a woman, smooth of features, long of hair, faultless of figure. Upon her exquisitely chiselled face was an extraordinary expression of frozen horror. She was half reaching forward, desperation expressed in every line. One slender arm was outthrust as if she were trying to get at something just beyond reach.

Opposite her, his back towards her, was an obviously young man with his stone hands resting on two stone switches. Above him were marvellously modelled tubes and condensers, wires, panels, and switches. On the floor beside him was an overturned stone bowl.

"Nice tableau, eh?" Bob asked, though he looked deeply puzzled.

"Nice enough, yes...." Mona ran a finger along her lips pensively as she contemplated the figures. "It's all so queer, though. Whoever made these models must have been a scientist as well. And a scientist-sculpture is a combination I've never even heard of."

Bob looked about him and then shrugged. "Well, I'm not very good at riddles, Mona—and anyway our job is to find a way back home. We've some concentrated food and drink in that wrecked plane of yours, but there's no telling how long it will last. At least our air should keep sweet for a long time with all this area to help us. Let's be seeing what else there is."

They continued walking and in every direction the torch flashed on more stone machinery of the same flawless designing, There were more figures too—some lying flat, others standing, all of them uncannily exact. The curious thing was that none of them were on pedestals. Also, unlike ordinary sculptures, the eyes were not left blank but were minutely filled in to give the impression of iris and pupil. Another significant point was that each one of the statues was turned so that it faced the distant switchboard at which the statue of the young man was seated.

"Apparently, there's no way out," Bob growled finally, as they came back to their starting point. It looks like we...."

He stopped, frowning as he studied the apparatus near the switchboard.

"Say," he muttered, "unless I'm plain crazy, that is intended to be a model of a telescopic reflector! I'd know one anywhere."

Going over to it, he studied its trellised length reaching up to the stony roof. Every part of it was perfect, representing without doubt a reflector not altogether dissimilar to 'Tiny' at Mount Wilson.

"For some reason," Mona said slowly, "I've got the returning conviction that I've seen this place before. I told you I felt that way even in the valley. But *here*...! She looked about her with a certain quality of awe. "This place is amazingly like the one I saw when I had that giddy spell a week or so back. Remember, I told you I had a flashing vision? I'll be hanged if I can understand all this. Surely nobody would go to the trouble of sculpting all this just for a hobby?"

"Great heavens!" Bob exclaimed. "Look!"

He pointed to another stone mechanism adjoining the reflector.

"So what?" Mona asked. "What's one model more than another?

"Don't you understand?" he insisted. "It's an almost exact replica of my projector! Just as it would have looked on a big scale had it ever got beyond being smashed."

"I'm sorry you had to bring that up," Mona commented. "I honestly don't know what made me...."

"Never mind that now; it's forgotten. Say, look at those two remote control pillars and the generator."

"Time I had a closer inspection," Mona decided.

She swung round, so suddenly that she forgot the stone statue of the woman close beside her. Though she made a vain effort to catch it, it heeled over and smashed on to the floor. An arm broke off and chippings flew out of the body.

"That's right, smash up the happy home!" Bob growled, "Why can't you be more careful...?"

"Say, there's something queer here," Mona interrupted him. Her tone was baffled as she picked up the broken piece of arm and studied it.

"What's queer about it?"

"The fact that the sculptor who made this even went far: enough to model interior muscle and bone! Or has my knowledge of physiology gone haywire?"

"But that's absurd! Impossible!"

Bob strode over and took the arm from Mona.

Carefully he examined the broken end. Inside there was certainly a perfect stone replica of bone, cartilage, and muscle. Bob dropped the thing suddenly as though it were a hot brick.

"Gosh!" he whistled blankly. "No sculptor would do that. He only needs the external, not internal, impression. If what I think is correct— Here, wait a moment!"

He levered the statue up from the floor and then swung it over again forcibly. It broke completely this time. He and Mona began a second and more extensive examination, then looked at each other grimly when they had finished.

"I was right!" Bob whispered. "Once upon a time— God knows how long ago—this was a living woman! She turned into stone! It gives you the jitters to think of it!"

"B—but how could any woman get like this?" Mona demanded. "Are you suggesting that someone just stood here with arm outflung whilst somebody poured liquid concrete over her, or something? Be yourself, Bob!"

"Listen Mona, this is no time for cracks," he said quietly. "And even assuming your cockeyed idea of liquid concrete to be correct, it wouldn't work. She would only get that on the outside of her body.... No, something happened here, which turned her inside and outside, her whole body, into stone. Queer, flaky sort of stone, too. Something quick and yet infinitely devastating which halted her in mid-action as she crossed this hall...."

"Rather like Lot's wife, eh, when she became a pillar of salt? On that assumption then," Mona continued, with a somewhat nervous look around her, "all these people here were once real and got petrified in some way?"

"Right! That's the way I figure it, anyhow."

Silence. Dusty immensity. Mystery.

"Under its stone covering," Bob resumed presently, "everything here must actually be normal. The switch-boards, the telescope, that apparatus which looks like my projector.... But what turned everything into stone?"

"Don't look at me: I wasn't there...." Mona paused and her forehead creased. "At least I don't think I was."

"Eh?" Bob swung and stared at her.

"I—I mean I can't figure it out, Bob. I keep getting odd twinges of memory."

"Which isn't much use to us," Bob decided. "I'm going to look further."

Moving across to the switchboard he kicked at it. The stone covering was little more than a barnacle-like surface, which shattered off under his repeated blows. Porcelain switches and devices came into view, unharmed, protected by the covering through untold generations.

Presently he turned to look at Mona. She was standing nearby, watching intently.

"There's a chance we might be able to do some-thing if we can get these switches to function," he said. "We'll try, anyway. If everything is protected by a stone coating, there's a chance it might still work. Give me a hand, will you?"

Mona nodded and lent prompt assistance. At the end an hour they had the switchboard comparatively free. He gently lifted aside the stone image of the young man and then sat in his place, gripping the same two switches. He hesitated noticeably.

"Jitters?" Mona enquired.

"Sort of," he muttered. "Something about this that sort of gets me. I feel as though I'm about to complete some sort of action which began in the mists of antiquity and was interrupted through unknown agencies...."

"How about skipping the poetry and pulling something?"

"All I'm likely to pull is a boner," Bob sighed; then with effort he closed one switch after another. They were stiff, but they worked.

Stone shards chipped off around the switch blades... then out of the silence there carne a low humming note. It jerked and quivered once or twice, then it rose to a clear rhythmic sound. Immediately Bob jumped out of his chair and with Mona at his side raced across to the source of the noise, found a stone-modelled dynamo humming steadily, shaking off its stone coveting with steady vibration.

"Well, I'll be damned!" Bob exclaimed. "Where does it get its power from, anyway? Unless...." He swung to a neighbouring machine composed of two vast cylinders reaching roofwards. There were a variety of stony dials upon which—though they did not make sense to him—were none-the-less registering!

"The power's coming from here!" he cried. "Can you beat that? Must be batteries or something...."

"Batteries! Lasting all these generations?"

Bob amended his statement quickly. "Well, storage batteries of some kind—perhaps solar power. How do we know how scientific these people were? We've partially exploited solar power ourselves for years. These folks could have improved upon it, maybe— Hello! What's happening now?"

He and Mona stood watching, fascinated, as amidst a rumbling roar of flying stone chippings the mighty telescopic reflector began to turn slowly on its universal mountings.

"So *that* was what that guy at the switchboard was doing last," Bob exclaimed. "Studying something through the reflector—and even now it is turning to that something by automatic control. Let's see what we get."

"Nothing, I expect," Mona said. "Unless it can see through a blank wall."

"You never know. Come on—let's watch this at close quarters."

After a while the reflector ceased its turning, obviously finishing at a predetermined point. Bob studied it for a moment, then looked at the stone-covered mirror. With extreme care he went to work with his knife to prise the stuff off, but even at that he cracked the delicate surface beneath, leaving only one clear portion undistorted. In that portion there was reflected a single star, surrounded by fainter ones. The solitary one glowed with a baleful lustre.

"Then this thing does penetrate rock!" he cried. "X-ray telescopy—and that star there is Sirius! Sirius... again." And his voice sobered.

He turned and found Mona stared at it fixedly. She caught the rail round the mirror for support.

"Yes—Sirius." Her voice was quivering. "I—I begin to understand something, Bob...something I might have understood beside 'Tiny' that night had I not fainted...."

"You all right?" Bob asked anxiously, holding her. "Not dizzy again?"

"No, no—just sort of fuzzy. I...." Mona paused, standing rigid. "A memory stream!" she breathed, her voice becoming trance-like. "The longer I gaze at Sirius, the more I can sense that which has been so long forgotten. I seem to be going down into some kind of gulf—listen, Bob...*listen*!"

CHAPTER FOUR

The city lay in the floor of a deeply shelving valley—a city of white stone built massive block upon
massive block, each section raised into position by
engineering processes destined to provide a riddle for
less intelligent races as yet undreamed of on the face
of the Earth.

The inhabitants of this city were the only beings in
the world—masters of science, light-centuries distant
from their own planet, and engaged upon an exploration
of the universe. The third world from the primary had
been singled out as worth of examination. Its murky
swamps and dense atmosphere, the titanic forests, the
roaming of colossal monsters—all these and more
offered plenty of interest to a race of intellectuals bent
on adding to their already vast store of knowledge.

Around the perfectly planned city the enormous
forest cloaked the mountainsides, reaching only as
far along the valley floor as the scientists permitted.
Otherwise the chasm between the mountain sides was
dear, a masterpiece of cross-sectioned roads, high
terraces, exquisitely beautiful buildings—all of it
soaked by day in a torrid equatorial sun which shone

fitfully through rents in boiling clouds, or illuminated by night with endless clusters of cold-light globes.

Over the destinies and scientific accomplishments of the city's inhabitants there ruled Cafna Brodix, quite eight centuries of age, yet with every faculty as alert as that of a young man. Science had found the way to indefinitely prolong life, but it still balked at defeating death. One day, a time must come....

On a particular evening, in the second year of the city's establishment in the valley, Cafna Brodix summoned the young man whom he considered one of the ablest scientists in the community—Cal Vandos by name, eighty-six years of age, yet looking and feeling as callow as a man of twenty-five.

He came into the ruler's private apartment as the western sky was chaotic with vermilion and amethyst flame above the treetops of the virgin forest. Cafna Brodix sat brooding at his desk, thrown into silhouette, seeming a perfect patriarch with his flowing, chest-deep white beard and easy Grecian-style raiment. He looked as Moses would one day look, centuries after these masterminds had been forgotten.

"You summoned me, Highest?" Cal Vandos asked quietly, pausing at the desk. He was good-looking, black-haired, with deep blue eyes and the slender, power-packed body of an athlete.

The man at the desk gave a little start and removed his gaze from the sunset. He turned a face that was heavily lined with the centuries of his living, yet the teeth were still firm, the eyes still bright, the expression one of immense wisdom and tolerance. His head, framed in a mane of white hair, was round with lofty temples. A nose, hooked as an eagle's gave him an air of irresistible power.

"I did, Cal," he assented quietly. "Please sit down."

The young scientist obeyed and waited respectfully. He showed no impatience as the ruler again pondered and the shadows darkened across the wild landscape of this young world. Impatience was unknown in most of the younger members of the race; complete nervous control made any irrational behaviour impossible. Life was of the quality of a smoothly flowing, unvarying river.

"It would seem," Cafna Brodix said at last, "that our examination of this young planet is about at its end. For two years now I have been receiving a constant flow of reports, all of them containing the necessary scientific data. And I much regret to say that our time has been more or less wasted."

"Wasted?" Cal looked surprised. "I should hardly have thought it possible for scientists to waste their time. Everything we discover, no matter how prosaic it may be, has a vital significance from the scientific point of view."

The ruler smiled in his beard and it made his tawny eyes seem brighter.

"You are a true scientist, Cal—but when you attain greater wisdom and years, you will realize that going over old ground and learning things already known is a tremendous waste of energy and talent...." He sighed and looked out towards the stars, which glinted occasionally between the drifting layers of cloud. "Nothing of real interest has been found here," he continued listlessly. "This world is more or less a facsimile of what our own world once was when it was very young."

There was silence in the massive, white-walled chamber. A gentle breeze came through the glassless frame of the giant window and stirred the fine metal records on the ruler's desk. It was coolly refreshing after the battering heat of the day hours.

"We travelled over twenty light-centuries to reach this planet because we thought it could give us something worthwhile," the ruler mused. "What a pitiful waste!"

Cal, ruled by logic as became his profession, gave a little shrug.

"Certainly we made a tremendous journey, Highest," he agreed; "but how is it possible to explore *any* world without visiting it? To rely on telescopic data alone is impossible—and indeed, even our science isn't capable of creating a telescope powerful enough to reach an infinite distance into space."

"True, true." The ruler spoke from abysmal shadow. He was a magnificently bearded silhouette against the stars: then a switch closed under his lean hand, and cold-light globes casting no trace of shadow suddenly turned the chamber to the brilliance of day. Cal Vandos blinked a little at the abrupt transition, and waited.

"When we started from our home world," the ruler continued, naming a planet near far-flung Aldebaran, "we had in mind the exploration of a certain area of the universe. We intended to chart a path through the universe and understand that path from end to end—just as some of our fellows travelled in the opposite direction with the same object in view. In a sense we became eternal wanderers, insofar that not one of the original explorers can possibly survive the entire exploration. The only people to ever return home will be the—as yet—unborn.

"But, and this is the vital point, we did not reckon with the fact that we might stumble on worlds wherein there was nothing to be learned, such as this one. Because of that we have spent endless years in a space-cruiser, making a journey wherein the time could have been put to much better use. In almost every respect there is little to choose between this world and our own, as it once was. The air is made up in similar proportions; the gravitation is identical; and from what we have forecasted of primeval life, it is possible the people who will finally populate this planet will be very much like us in formation. So, what have we gained? Not knowledge, my young friend. Not experience. And since those are the only two factors worthy of admission, we can only have gained precisely—nothing!"

Cal nodded slowly, thinking. "Seen from that standpoint, Highest, I have to agree with you," he admitted.

"So we must guard against a repetition of this mistake." The ruler became suddenly earnest, resting his arms on the desk and interlacing his fingers. "We already have it planned to visit the other planets in this system and see what they hold. Certainly the journeys would not be great—mere millions of miles as compared to light-centuries on the trip we made here; but I insist that there must be no more time loss. We must know ahead which are the best worlds to visit, which can improve our knowledge. That, as you yourself remarked, demands much more than telescopic observation."

"You have some theory in mind?" Cal questioned.

"No, I have not even attempted to work on the matter. I only came to the conclusion that we are wasting our time after looking through the reports this evening. I sent for you to put the problem in your hands. I know your skill, your untiring energy. You will devise something by which we can know ahead if a planet is worth the energy of visiting it."

"Have I a time limit for planning this out?" Cal asked.

"No, that would warp your creative genius. No creator can work to a fixed rule. All I ask is that you find something within a reasonable period and submit your theory—or even a model if you can make one—to me."

Cal Vandos nodded and rose. "I will do my utmost, Highest—and thank you for having such faith in me."

"It is not misplaced," the ruler smiled, and bowed the young scientist from the chamber.

In the big, air-cooled corridor outside the ruler's sanctum, Cal stood thinking and frowning for a while. Though it pleased him immeasurably to have the ruler's complete confidence, there was also the other side to think of something worthy of that confidence.

Musing, Cal presently continued on his way down the vista, emerging at length on to the terrace. When he had crossed the paved quadrangle, he came to the massive stone rail. Hands upon it, he stood gazing into the night. Here on the terrace there were no lights. It was used for those who wished the solitude of the night in which to ponder, or converse in low tones. The bulk of the lighted building nearby was not so close that it forced itself upon the senses.

"A problem," Cal Vandos muttered, drawing in deep breaths of the cool night wind. "A problem indeed...."

His voice carried further than he had anticipated. It reached the ears of a slender girl who was just advancing on to the terrace from its further end. She was fairly tall, and moved with a grace which was a symphony in itself, her fair hair flowing unbridled to her shoulders, the soft wind moulding the delicate white garments to her flawless figure as she moved. When she came to the side of the young scientist, she spoke softly—and he gave a start.

"What is it, Cal, that is such a problem?" she questioned, and leaned back against the rail to study his serious face in the starlight.

"Nothing that need worry you, Onia." He caught her shoulders gently and kissed her smiling face. "Just a little mystery that the Highest has posed for me."

"The Highest?" Onia was vaguely visible as she expressed surprise. "I should have thought the Highest could solve all his own mysteries."

"He can, but occasionally he hands them on to the less experienced to see what they are made of. I've just come from him. He is bemoaning the fact that we crossed twenty light-centuries to no purpose. Not that you or I have any recollection of ever leaving our home planet, since we were born on the space-cruiser; but it seems to worry him quite a lot."

The wide blue eyes of Onia Linida, daughter of Kio Linida, the chief mathematician of the expedition, turned and looked at the sky centring at last on an infinitesimal speck of reddish light swallowed in the deeps of heaven, all but swamped indeed by the glare of mightier luminaries.

"To think that is our sun!" she whispered. "How strange it seems, Cal. How utterly, fantastically strange! To be descended from a race inhabiting a world we have never seen and never shall."

"It doesn't affect me that way," Cal answered, smiling.

"Space and this world have been our homes.... However, as I was saying, the Highest considers we have lost valuable time, so to me he has handed the unenviable job of devising a method whereby we can know exactly what to expect of any planet we visit."

Onia turned from studying the heavens to listen.

"The only thing I can imagine at the moment is some kind of projector," Cal said thoughtfully. "Something that can reach out into space ahead of us, moving as fast as light."

"Faster, surely?" the girl asked. "Assuming you wished to test an extremely distant planet—say one as far away as our home world—the speed of light would be too slow. It would take years to receive an answer."

"Yes, that's true. In that case there remains for me to work out a method by which the speed of light can be exceeded. I have never been able to understand why it shouldn't be, but of course the law is rigid when applied to the three dimensions of length, depth, and breadth. Now, were I to incorporate the still theoretical fourth and fifth dimensions, it is possible I...."

"Cal," the girl interrupted gently, "I am only the daughter of a mathematician, and I haven't the vaguest idea what you are talking about! When theories go beyond the known laws, I'm completely lost."

Cal laughed. "I'm inclined to forget that, dearest. One thing I do know—I wouldn't love you half so ardently if you were scientific. Many of the women in our race are, I know—but they're arid and uninteresting. To my mind a woman should always be a woman. No more, no less."

"Exacting, and yet I like it," Onia decided. "Anyway, if you can forget the wishes of the Highest for a moment, I came to discover if we are taking our usual walk this evening. Or has this problem put everything else out of your head?"

"Not to that extent," Cal assured her. "We've walked together every evening since we landed on this planet—and we'll go on doing it. What other chance do we get to discuss our plans for the time when we are permitted to marry?"

He took her arm possessively and they began to stroll across the terrace, presently descending twenty-eight massive white steps to the main street, which ran through the town's centre. Here the twilight was banished by the glow of shadowless cold light globes. Traffic, utterly silent, moved up and down the broad, specially designed tracks. On the pedestrian-way the people of the city, their scientific occupations ended for the day, were taking advantage of recreation. There was a variety of things they could do—but this time Cal's mind at least shied from the relaxation of amusement. Finally, preoccupied, he steered Onia into one of the broad, softly lighted parks They seated themselves in the warm dusk beneath the vastly spreading branches of a giant conifer.

"Nothing else for it, Onia, but for me to see your father." Cal said at length, and the girl looked at him in surprise.

"About us, do you mean? Concerning our forthcoming marriage?"

"Great heavens, no! That is decided by laws and regulations and the Council of Eugenics. I mean in regard to the problem I have on hand. It'll need the brains of an expert to work out the mathematics of the fourth and fifth dimensions. I—er...." Cal hesitated. "I'm not sure, though, how your father will take it."

"It's a problem, isn't it? He thrives on them!"

"Yes, but he's a believer in every scientist solving his own problems. He told me some time ago, when he knew that you and I were planning to marry, that he considered it essential I should be intellectually worthy of you. Physically, we know we are correctly matched. I hope he won't think I'm falling down when I ask him for help. That might decide him block our marriage. As your parent he has that privilege...."

"You are worrying needlessly, Cal," the girl responded. "I know father seems pretty fierce some-times, but it's only his way. Actually, he is one of the kindest of men."

"Mmm. Well. Could you sort of prepare him in advance for my visiting him? I propose to call tomorrow morning at his headquarters A little work on your part beforehand might do a world of good. I don't want to take any risk which might disturb our future."

Onia's hand stole out and gripped Cal's gently. "Rely on it, I'll pave the way for you. You'll find father entirely tractable when you meet him tomorrow."

* * * * * * *

It was ten o'clock the following morning when Cal knocked gently on the shining doors of the sanctum assigned to Kio Linida, the chief mathematician. A voice boomed forth from beyond.

"Come in, come in! Don't stand tapping!"

Cal entered, closed the door quietly, then marched across the waste of floor. The chief mathematician was at his desk, alone, writing busily in a blazing shaft of sunlight through the glassless window. In the roof a fan whirred gently.

"I thought it would be you," Linida said finally, and threw down his electrical calculating instrument. "Onia told me you'd be scared to see me."

"I'm not scared!" Cal protested. "It's just that I...."

"Sit down!" Linida ordered.

Cal did so and frowned somewhat. His eyes remained on the mathematician. Kio Linida was fearsome-looking because his eyebrows were massive sandy tufts descending in a V-formation to an amazingly hooked nose. He had always chosen to remain clean-shaven, which left him with a craggy face and jutting lips and chin. This effect, combined with his piercing blue eyes and powerful voice, had earned for him the reputation of a despot.

"Well?" he demanded. "What in cosmos are you looking so dismal about, boy? You'll have to be a good deal more cheerful when you are married to Onia or there'll be trouble. I can't stand morose people!" He laughed roughly; then his eyes became gimlet-sharp again. "Speak up!" he commanded.

"I am carrying out an order from the Highest," Cal explained. "Or at least I am trying to. He...."

"...wants you to find a means of exploring planets before we get there. Yes, yes, I know. Onia told me. Queer thing is that she got the facts right. Shouldn't have thought it of her. Confoundedly empty-headed sometimes, like her mother used to be. Don't know how she pins down her job as laboratory-assistant. So, having no ideas of your own, you've come to me for some, eh? And intend taking the credit too, I suppose?"

"Not at all, sir!" Cal could not be angry even had he wanted. He belonged to a later school than Kio Linida, a school which had all emotional tendencies ironed out from birth. In some ways the mathematician was a throwback—an ordinary human being.

"Don't sit there arguing with me, boy!" Linida snorted, and banged his fist on the desk. "You wouldn't be here if you didn't want something. Can't be my daughter; you've got her—and by the cosmos I admire your choice. But...."

"I don't know whether Onia told you or not," Cal broke in, "but all I need from you is the mathematical set-up of the fourth and fifth dimensions."

The mathematician's boring eyes narrowed. "Oh, that's it, is it? You are sure you wouldn't like the ninth integral calculus as a makeweight?"

Cal looked rather helpless for a moment; then his expression changed to astonishment as the mathematician suddenly burst forth into a gale of laughter. He shook with mirth, lips writhing back from faultless teeth.

"By the beard of the Highest, I do believe you're effeminate, Cal!" he exclaimed; then the smile had gone and the worried look was back on his face. "Why don't you tell me I'm a noisy old fool, and have done with it?"

"I certainly do think that this problem is worth more than your laughter and contempt," Cal answered, without any alteration in the pitch of his voice—and his remark brought a new light into the mathematician's eyes.

"That's more like it!" he cried. "Giving me as good as I send! Yes, you'll do! I couldn't stand Onia being married to a man who bowed down to everything I told him. *Defy* me! That's it! And I'll have endless pleasure breaking you if you dare try it! Mmm, so you want the facts on the fourth and fifth dimensions, do you? Why?"

"So I can work out a system which can defeat the speed of light. I don't believe it is actually the binding factor of the universe."

Linida sat back in his chair and mused, his eyes vanishing into the monstrous tufts covering them.

"I think you are right," he said finally. "The speed of light is only an arbitrarily defined term, like the length of a day. I have myself worked out various theoretical formulae to show that light is not the ultimate speed. But, if I devise the necessary basic mathematics, to what use do you intend to put them?"

"I have an idea concerning a projector, sir. As far as I can see it is the only possible way to put the Highest's order into effect."

As the mathematician waited for elaboration Cal reached inside his tunic and brought forth a roll of wafer-thin metal. He laid it out on the desk for Linida to study.

"There it is, sir—a rough design of my projector. You will observe that it is entirely automatic and fitted inside with devices which will cut rock and minerals, withdraw air and water samples, and generally take unto itself the ingredients of a distant world or sun. It can be despatched by force beams and withdrawn by magnetic ones, radio being used throughout for its guidance. That system, checked constantly by astronomical instruments, would mean that this projector could go anywhere and come back, bringing samples with it. I call it a 'projector' because that is what it actually is: it projects ahead of that which will follow."

"Umph," the chief mathematician said, stroking a craggy neck and considering. "The idea's good, boy. Presumably you want the 'faster-than-light' mathematics so that you can make this thing cover a vast distance in as short a time as possible?"

"That's it, sir." Cal was obviously relieved at not having to explain further. He allowed the plan to roll up again and returned it to his tunic. "As you are aware, I am purely and simply a scientist, with a Class A mathematical knowledge. With you it is different. You have made mathematics your life's work, so I have come to you. All our computing devices are robots: they can calculate anything to a split fraction, but they cannot think out a new theory. Only you can do that."

"Nice to know that I am useful for something," Linida growled. "I seem to spend most of my time thinking out abstruse formulae which never lead anywhere. Yes, this is really worthwhile!" He clapped his big hands together vigorously. "All right, son, I'll go to work on it and let you have the formulae the moment I've worked them out. However...there is one thing...."

Cal waited, somewhat surprised. He asked a question as Linida sat scowling.

"You mean a mistake of some kind, sir?"

"Hardly a mistake. Your scientific planning for the projector is impeccable, boy—impeccable. But you are not over wise in some things. For instance"—the piercing eyes became bright with interrogation—"how do you know what you will get when you withdraw materials from other planets, or suns?"

"I don't, sir. That's the whole point of trying."

"Dangerous gamble," Linida rumbled, shaking his head. "Suppose, just as a theory, you withdrew from some world a deadly type of creature? What do you imagine would happen when you opened up your portable laboratory? You might be struck dead, driven mad—anything! Or on the other hand, suppose you extracted from some world a form of explosive atmosphere which, upon you opening the ampule, set fire to the oxygen-nitrogen content of this planet? All possibilities, boy—grim possibilities. You're playing a very dangerous game."

"That is possibly something the Highest has not considered." Cal admitted. "However, I'll take every precaution. I'll have robot devices to unload the projector when it returns from its journey."

"Good enough," Linida answered, satisfied. "Now you can leave me to work in peace. Be off with you!"

Cal promptly went, only too glad to be relieved of the mathematical responsibility. He was halfway down the corridor on his way to the outdoors when he came suddenly upon Onia. Evidently she had been waiting for him in one of the big stone recesses.

"Well?" she asked eagerly, as Cal put an affectionate arm about her shoulders. "What happened?"

"Everything's all right. I'm satisfied, Onia, that your father sounds a lot fiercer than he really is. He was most helpful—and will continue to be so. He gave me a warning, too, concerning something of which I'd never thought...." Briefly Cal told the girl of the sinister possibilities which might ensue from extracting something from an alien world.

"That won't stop you, though, will it?" she asked.

"It hasn't got to. The Highest is expecting results, and he'll lave to have them. I don't anticipate any trouble."

Onia was silent. She still had not spoken by the time she and Cal had reached the outdoors and the hot glare of the street.

"Something the matter?" Cal enquired, and she looked up at him quickly.

"Not—really." She hesitated. "Just that my father is so wise. He has a gift for scenting trouble before it arrives. Now he has given you such a grave warning, I really do wish the Highest had never given you such an order. If you *did* happen to draw something incredibly dangerous from another world, it might mean the end of us."

Cal laughed. "Have no fear, dearest; I know exactly what I'm doing. I mean to take all precautions...." He changed the subject as he saw Onia's troubled expression. "How did you manage to get here and meet me? You ought to be at work in the laboratory, surely?"

"I slipped out. I just had to know how you had got on with father,"

"Well the sooner you slip back to work, the better. It's safest to obey regulations."

Onia nodded, smiling again through the dim fear at the back of her thoughts.

"I'll go," she said. "And I'll see you as usual tonight."

Cal kissed her lightly and watched her hurry away along the almost deserted pedestrian way. Then he turned his footsteps in the direction of the laboratories. It annoyed him to find that he too was worried now. It had never occurred to him—or presumably to Cafna Brodix—that to extract materials from unknown worlds might be a short cut to major disaster.

"I must take care," he muttered to himself. "I *must*!"

CHAPTER FIVE

Three days later—days in which Cal worked on the construction of his projector, assisted by a small band of experts assigned to the making of different components—the chief mathematician had finished his formulae.

When he came to examine them, Cal did not even pretend to understand them, involving as they did all the laws of higher mathematics. His alternative was to feed the tables of figures to the mathematical computing machines and leave them to sort them out, a system which worked admirably and enabled him finally to set about the construction of a separate mathematical-computer to be linked to the radio-magnetic equipment controlling the projector. With this computer he could set the required course and estimate the time it would take the projector to cover it—allowing the divergencies through fourth and fifth dimensions by which the limiting factor of light became no longer operative.

In the main, Cal was working in the dark, and readily admitted the fact to his fellow technicians. He knew what the fourth and fifth dimensions accomplished, but how they did it was beyond him. And Linida, though he knew all the secrets—and sometimes came to super-vise progress—did not divulge anything. The more mathematical mysteries he kept to himself, the more indispensable became his position in the community.

A fortnight passed before Cal was ready to make his first experiment and, in the presence of the Highest himself, Linida, and one or two other members of the ruling clique, he sent his projector to the nearest world and back in the space of five minutes. The planet that would one day be called Mars and be known as a red and barren world, now yielded samples of its terrain and atmosphere.

"Splendid, splendid!" the Highest declared, when the mechanical analyzers had checked over the various items.

"That world forty-five million miles distant is obvi-ously on a par with this one, except that it is long past its peak and is in severe decline. Its air is almost gone, leaving it open to meteoric bombardment, and its oceans have long since evaporated. We could have wasted a good deal of time going there, only to discover that any life it might once have held is long since extinct. I think we can rule that world out of our calculations and seek others."

The assembly of scientists looked at each other and nodded. Then Cafna Brodix glanced towards Cal as he stood waiting.

"Test the other planets in this system, Cal," the ruler instructed. "If one of them yields something really interesting, making it worthy of a visit, advise me.

If not, then probe further afield—as much so as you wish, just as long as we come to a world or system where there is scope for our talents."

"I will do that, Highest," Cal promised, and, satisfied that he could be left to the task, the scientists departed from the laboratory....

From that moment onwards Cal knew exactly what he had to do—and did it. Constantly, when his normal laboratory work did not demand his attention, he sent the projector back and forth, each time making a careful analysis of the substances and air-ampules brought back. From the inner planets he derived nothing more of interest. From the world nearest the sun he obtained only pulverized rock and barely a trace of any atmospheric content at all.

From the giants furthest from the luminary, there came ampules of pure ammonia-gas in high proportion—worlds obviously useless for colonization and exploration; and from the very furthest dwarf planet, small but heavy, there came a pure carbon-like substance of considerable heaviness. Altogether, it appeared that the immediate system of planets was hardly worth attention.

So Cal reached further. Accustomed by now to his apparatus, he spent many hours examining the heavens, trying to decide on a particular star, which might have interesting planets circling around it.

It was a vivid yellow binary which finally attracted his attention. The X-ray telescopic devices with which he worked made the almost incessant night clouds as transparent as glass, and, time and again, amongst all the hosts of heaven there was no binary which fascinated him so much as this yellow steadily glowing monster, with a much smaller star well below fifth magnitude dancing constant attendance on the majestic giant.

Cal made no attempt to use his projector until he had gathered all the necessary information concerning the binary, and this he communicated to the Highest in an interview.

"I really believe, Highest, that we may have something unusual here, Cal explained. "You will see from these photographic plates that the star is double—yet the fifth-magnitude attendant, though small, is half as massive in density as the giant himself. The two together make up a mass three and a half times that of the sun in this system we now occupy."

"Most interesting," the Highest commented, thinking. "I do not think that in all our investigations we have yet come across so singular an occurrence. Densely heavy matter, presumably, on the part of the smaller star. I note here that the big star is twice as massive as the sun in this system, and sixty-five times as brilliant; whereas the smaller star has only one one-sixtieth of the light of this system's sun, yet equals him in mass.... Yes, Cal, I am interested."

"To the best of my knowledge, sir, there are planets in this binary system," Cal continued. "At this distance of 8.7 light years I cannot actually see them, but there are perturbations which, mathematically, can only be explained as planetary orbits. Since these planets cannot be pinpointed, I'm unable to send my projector to them and withdraw samples, but I can send the projector to the giant star and his attendant. Since any system of planets derives its materials from the primary—the sun—it seems to me that the elements of these dual suns will be repeated in the planets. If any substance which is useful to us should be revealed, it might be worth a journey for closer examination,"

"By all means proceed," Cafna Brodix assented, "and report your results. How long do you suppose it will take your projector to travel the distance to travel there and back to this star system?"

"About six hours, sir—twelve to both stars, using the fourth and fifth dimensions to foreshorten space."

The ruler nodded. "Excellent! I shall await your report with eagerness."

Cal bowed his way out and returned to the laboratory. He was feeling happier than for many months. At last he had something worthy of experimentation, and perhaps it would bring to an end the useless probing and testing of planets that were nothing more than worthless rock. For instance, densely heavy matter might contain valuable ores specially needed in the building of long-life scientific equipment.

The main thing now was to plan the course accurately—a job for the mathematical machines. The extreme eccentricity of the giant star and his associate, separated from each other by a mean distance of some 2,000 million miles, would mean vastly different courses for the radio and magnetic waves guiding the projector. The whole process indeed was extremely involved—a mosaic of arithmetical planning being needed which would probably have defeated even Linida himself.

Not so the machines. They began clicking away at the problem the moment Cal fed the root-figures into their matrices. Then he sat back to await the results which would show him exactly what numbers to set on the indicator.

A sound behind him, above the hum of the mathematical monsters, made him turn. It was Onia who entered the laboratory, moving as usual as though a gentle breeze carried her.

"I know I've no right here," she confessed, as Cal gave her a rather stern look, "but we seem to have seen so little of each other lately. We no longer take our walks in the evenings. You always seem to be here. So, when I saw that most of the late staff had left for the night, I thought I'd risk coming in. After all, I have some right to do so, considering my father's position."

"And I'm only too glad to see you," Cal laughed, drawing her to him. "You've arrived at about the most exciting time, too."

"I have?" Her blue eyes widened. "How so?"

Cal gave her the details. She listened with absorbed interest and then her eyes travelled to the computers.

"And these are working out the individual courses to the star and its...little friend?"

"Exactly. Although they look nearly on top of each other in the telescope, the actual distance between them is some two thousand million miles, so of course the direction taken by the projector to the giant star will have to be very different from its attendant."

"Could I...see them?" Onia asked. "Through the telescope, I mean?"

"Surely...." Smiling, Cal took her arm and led her over to the giant instrument, motioning to the mirror-reflector as he switched on the apparatus. Fascinated, the girl stood and gazed at the mighty yellow giant with his duller yellow satellite.

"No name for him yet?" she asked presently.

"Not yet. They're known as L-4 and L-19. Numbers do equally well."

"I don't think so," Onia said, shaking her head. "Numbers for such beautiful stars seem too ordinary— especially for the big one. He's so huge, so scorching.... I think he ought to be called 'Sirius'. In our ancient language form that means 'burning'. Why not call the little star following him the 'Companion'? Surely that is what he is?"

"All right," Cal laughed. "If it makes you any happier. Even if the powers that be think names are superfluous, it doesn't stop you using them. Sirius and Companion it shall be...."

Cal broke off and turned quickly as the nearer mathematical computing machine suddenly ceased its whining. From it he extracted a thin metal printout and considered it, Onia looking over his shoulder.

"This is the course to Sirius himself," he explained. "The other machine is working out the track for the

Companion— Well, let's see what we get."

Turning to the projector, he made a final check over its many complexities, then transferred it to the chute which carried it to the transmission room on the upper floor of the laboratory. From here it would automatically be fired into space from a ramp on the building's summit, controlled thereafter by remote control radio.

To Onia, unaccustomed to the scientific wizardry of the laboratory, there was something fascinating about the matrix of keys before which Cal now seated himself, playing them as he might the console of a massive organ. For every switch and button he moved, a tube came into glowing colour-life and a display registered.

"This," he said, without glancing at Onia as she stood watching, "is quite the most exacting job of all! Having the numbers on the computer, which are matched from those of the other mathematical machines, my job is to keep them constantly in alignment. That makes certain that the projector will reach Sirius without trouble via the fourth and fifth dimensions. It will be a long job, though. To cover 8.7 light years takes six hours."

"It is only seven o'clock as yet," Onia said, glancing at the clock. "Father's on night duty and I've nothing much to do—so I'll stay here even if it is until the early hours. This is too exciting to miss."

Cal nodded and said nothing, his attention fixed on the equipment.

"One thing I don't understand," Onia resumed presently. "So far you have sent your projector to planets and obtained substances from them—but in this case you are sending it to a brilliantly hot star, a mighty sun. What do you hope to get from it? Won't its very mass and heat destroy the projector?"

"No. The projector is so devised that when it comes near to something of critical temperature, which might destroy it, it will go no further. The mechanisms lock and the radio beams can no longer drive it forward—a fact that is registered on these dials here. In this case I calculate that the projector will cease to advance when it reaches the outermost fringe of Sirius' atmosphere. But the projector's internal apparatus will function and draw off a sample of that atmosphere. That will be all we need. The constitution of any planet is identical to that of its sun, except that it has everything in the solid form instead of the gaseous. From the gaseous samples we'll know what to expect of any planets in that system. There *are* planets, but to calculate their positions and send the projector to them is next to impossible."

Onia nodded slowly, though she looked as if she did not fully understand the intricacies; then she glanced towards the second mathematical computer as it clicked and printed out its findings..

"The course for the Companion," Cal said, without looking up. "Take it out of the print slot, Onia, and put it on one side ready for later on."

Glad to be of assistance, the girl did as she was bidden, and for a while studied the endless columns of baffling symbols. Finally she gave them up as beyond her and set the sheet on one side.... So there began for both she and Cal a long and wearying wait. It was particularly exacting for Cal in that he dared not relax for a moment, for fear a miscalculation arose on the matrix keyboard which, multiplying with the other groups of interlocking figures, would throw the whole thing out balance and lose him the projector somewhere in the deeps of space.

Ten o'clock came, and shortly after it his instruments told him the projector had reached the limit of its journey. He promptly cut out the force-beams and switched on the magnetic sequence. The effect on the incredibly distant projector, poised between dimensions within close proximity to Sirius, would be to commence drawing it back through the deeps of space. For this no guidance was necessary. The projector would come back to its starting point, the transmission room in the upper chamber of the laboratory.

Eleven and twelve o'clock passed. Cal kept himself awake with an effort. Coiled up in a chair, Onia was half dozing. Then towards one o'clock there came a dull click in the mechanisms. Immediately Cal sat up intently and considered the readings. All of them were at zero.

"Onia!" He got up quickly and went over to her, shaking her shoulder. "Onia, time's up! It's returned!"

She looked at him through sleepy eyes for a moment, then as she fully realized what he meant, she got up hastily and followed him to the narrow stairway leading to the upper region.

Here she slowed her pace, as a few yards away, Cal

stood considering the projector through the radiation-proofed, transparent walls of the transmission-room. This was a small booth sealed off from the chamber proper, in which lay the projector,

It was shaped like a shell, with tapering ends, and had plainly suffered a good deal of exposure to heat in its weird trip. Its densely thick outer covering was scored and pitted from the flaming furies it had encountered near Sirius.

"Well, let's see what it brought back," Cal said at last, moving to the switchboard beside the booth, then by way of explanation he added: "This sealed room is to protect us in case something unpleasant emerges from the projector. Nothing can get through these transparent walls except ordinary light, so we're safe."

He closed a switch. The head of the projector opened under magnetic impulses and from within it there was ejected a scaled ampule. Nothing more. Usually small rocks and any possible plants were also tossed forth, but not this time. Just the ampule, and this was filled to its automatically sealed top with a cloudy purplish gas.

"A terrific journey just for this!" Onia sighed. "What do you suppose it is?"

"Presumably a sample of the gaseous envelope of Sirius—and just what we need. From analysis we can tell the constitution of the planets that circle him. And that's soon done."

Moving to the wall Cal wheeled over a complex analyzing equipment on rubber wheels. Fitting two electrode-like rods through special traps in the case, he clamped one to the top of the ampule and one to the bottom, then he switched on the power. Carefully he studied the analysis percentages the displays gave.

"Basically hydrogen," he said finally, "but there's also another gas of a type I don't recognize. Heavy, unstable stuff—and it might have dangerous qualities. Before I do anything, I'd better let the experts see it, including your father and the Highest. If there's nothing better from the Companion, I'm afraid the experiment won't have been worthwhile after all."

He pushed the analyzer back to the wall and then closed another switch on the panel. A brief blast of radiation was sufficient to shatter the ampule, leaving the gases free to float foggily about the transparent walls of the booth. Another switch ejected the projector through a vacuum trap. Taking care not to touch it, Cal used a small overhead crane to lever it into a second booth nearby.

"That's the way we do it," he explained, as he returned to Onia. "A separate transmission-room for each trip, both rooms mobile. As for this gas-filled one...."

He seized hold of the insulated rods projecting from it and wheeled it without effort across the polished floor until he came to a massive door sunken into the wall. A switch opened it—a door quite two feet thick and lead-sheathed. Onia watched as the booth was wheeled into the chamber beyond, then Cal withdrew and shut the door again.

Turning, he looked at the remaining transmission-booth in which the now re-closed projector lay ready for its transmission into space via the suction tube on top of the case—which in turn vanished into the roof.

"Everything okay," he decided. "Let's get back to the lab."

Onia went ahead of him down the stairway and stood on one side to watch as once more he settled in the control chair. His actions were more or less a replica of those he had performed when sending the projector to Sirius, except that on this occasion different numbers were used on the master-computer. Finally he had everything crosschecked, and switched on the power. The familiar buzzing note spread through the laboratory and he began his endless playing on the matrix keys.

"What do you suppose makes the Companion of Sirius so heavy, even though it is so small?" Onia asked presently, thinking.

"The only explanation is that it is a 'collapsed' star. It happens often. Some tremendous internal disturbance causes the outer photosphere to cave in, and the gaseous envelope contracts to under half its original size. Hence we get the effect of a body weighing as heavy as one twice its size."

Onia nodded vaguely and dropped the subject before it became too involved for her. Not that Cal had much opportunity to talk. His attention was riveted on the switchboard, and it more or less remained that way for three hours, until the instruments told him the projector had reached the Companion of Sirius. After that, with the projector being magnetically drawn back to Earth, he could afford to be less attentive.

It was dawn when the projector returned. Immediately Cal led the way upstairs, and when he had moved the switch that opened the projector's head, he and Onia stood gazing at yet another form of gas, sealed into its ampule. This time is was greyish and, after analyzing it, Cal shook his head dubiously.

"Not the vaguest idea what it is," he confessed. "It does not seem to have any hydrogen in it; or for that matter is it any gas we ever heard of. This ought to please the Highest, anyway. Something at last that is a mystery!"

"How do you set about discovering its properties?" Onia asked.

"That's a long job, and one which I certainly don't intend to attempt now. For the time being, this gas can go in the vault and we're going to our respective homes to try and get some sleep before daylight comes."

Cal did not smash the ampule and release the gas into the booth. Being unsure of its properties, it was a risk he did not care to take. He wheeled the transmission-room, the projector still inside it, into the vault and left it side by side with the neighbouring booth. This done he closed the huge door and time-locked it.

The long and tedious job of analysis could wait until later when he had a band of assistants round him and all needful precautions could be taken.

CHAPTER SIX

Cal arrived at the laboratory an hour later than his usual time the following morning. Not that it signified. After the all-night work upon which he had been engaged, a certain laxity was permissible, and he was more or less his own master.

Humming a tune to himself, cheerful in the knowledge that be had found a system unusual enough to please Cafna Brodix, he nodded cordially to the technical staff as he went on his way to the laboratory. Reaching it, he turned immediately to the massive door and looked at the time-lock. It was fifteen minutes beyond the period for which he had set it.

A movement on the controlling wheel and a snapping of switches set the mighty hinged barrier on the move. It swung outwards and Cal switched on the light, intending to stride into the vault's interior and look at the transmission-booth,

Instead he stopped dead, staring incredulously.

Something uncanny had happened. The booth that had contained the grey gas from the Companion of Sirius had been burst apart. Of grey gas there was no longer any trace. Instead a viscid, crawling substance, still remotely grey in colour, was flowing out of the smashed remains of the booth, multiplying on itself as it moved. In some blind, terrifying way it was alive. In the course of the few hours that had elapsed it had almost filled the vault, was clinging to the floor, walls, and ceiling. Now, with the door opened, it began to ooze outwards into the laboratory.

Just in time Cal jumped back, and a quivering, proto-plasmic grey tentacle slid, expanded, and shivered an inch from his feet. He licked his lips and stared, now noting something else. The plasmic effect was only operative where the stuff was flowing; otherwise it had metamorphosed into something granular, almost stone-like, and completely immovable. Of the booth that had contained the gas from Sirius itself, there was no sign, though its bulk was vaguely visible under the stuff.

These facts Cal absorbed in the space of a few seconds; then he made a sudden wild effort to shut the massive door—and failed completely. The stuff had flowed gummily into a ridge behind it and exerted so much living, crushing pressure that it was impossible to budge the door in the slightest. Beaten, Cal backed away, his eyes wide.

"What in cosmos is it?" he half whispered to himself.

For a moment he felt like running for it, or at least calling in the other scientists in the building to help him combat the stuff, then he remembered that the responsibility for this occurrence was entirely his. His mood changed to one of grim resolution to deal with the stuff.

Its nature he did not know. It was alive—a blind form of life which died nearly as fast as it moved, leaving behind a stony kind of substance. The thing to do was to destroy it before it got out of hand.

Dashing across to the bench he picked up a bottle of nitric acid, unstoppered it, and then flung it wholesale into the stuff. To his amazement nothing very remarkable happened. The stuff smoked and sizzled as the acid soaked in and an unbearable stench arose—but the dirty gleaming grey tendrils still reached and crawled towards the walls, along the floor, creeping with waving pseudopodia towards the equipment on the bench.

Still determined to master the thing, Cal whirled towards a distant wall of the laboratory where stood several flasks of liquid air, a pale blue fluid carefully stoppered. He rolled the centremost flask forward and with an effort heaved it into his arms—then he threw it with all his strength.

The flask splintered in the midst of the substance, striking the stony edges of the section that had ceased to move. The savagely cold fluid, biting enough to reduce steel itself to powder, sank into the plasma. It blackened quickly for an area, and Cal held his breath in wild hope—then he groaned to himself as after the black area had died and turned to hard grey shell, the remainder kept on moving, presumably growing on itself by fission.

It was brought home to him now with grim impact

that here indeed was something utterly unearthly. No substance with a normal understandable origin would have been able to absorb nitric acid and liquid air and still keep going.

Cal's gaze swept back to where the stuff was piling, flowing and oozing out of the strong room vault—then to the bench where the treacly tendrils were creeping upwards and investigating blindly, leaving behind them solid dead cells of deep stone grey. Something had to be done, and quickly. Cal swung to the laboratory doorway, intent on getting help. He stopped dead as Kio Linida, the chief mathematician, came striding through it.

Linida jerked to a halt, his massive eyebrows rising as he glared at the mystery substance spreading in all directions.

"By the beard of the Highest, what's this?" he demanded blankly, and his piercing eyes swung in enquiry to Cal.

"I'd give all I have to know, sir," Cal retorted, his alarm obvious. "Whatever it is, I can't stop it. It flowed out of the vault door when I opened it a few minutes ago."

Linida watched the stuff narrowly as he said: "Onia told me how she had spent the night watching you get stuff from L-4 and L-19—or Sirius and the Companion as she, for some fool reason, prefers to call them. I thought I'd come along and see about the rare gas she was talking about."

"As far as I know, this is the rare gas!" Cal replied.

"It's changed into a viscid solid overnight, but I haven't the least notion why."

"Tried killing it?" the mathematician snapped.

"Acid and liquid air, so far. Neither had any effect."

"Something has got to have!" Linida decided. "If this keeps on spreading—as it will, since it obviously divides and subdivides constantly—feeding on itself, *anything* might happen! Better see what a burst of radiation can do to it."

Thankful for the older man to take control, Cal surrendered himself to following out orders and lending assistance as different laboratory equipment was loosed on the ever-advancing stuff. Pure ultra violet and infrared radiations were hurled at it; so were supersonic beams. Then lights of twenty-million candle power were used in case it was sensitive to glare. Water was tried; even naked electrodes were flung into it with thousands of high-tension volts streaming through them....

To no avail. The stuff blackened and smudged in spots, but it progressed inexorably. An hour had passed by the time Cal and Linida had exhausted all the laboratory's resources. They stood gazing fixedly as the plasma crawled silently up the walls, covering the instruments, but not absorbing them. It became plain that the stuff more or less flowed over them, leaving the outline behind it in a greyish, hardened covering.

"We're up against it, boy," Linida said finally. "What in cosmos you have brought from Sirius I don't know, but we've got to find out. The only thing we can do is isolate a fragment of this stuff and analyze it somewhere in safety. The Highest must be informed of this immediately. First—a fragment."

The mathematician strode across the laboratory and searched amongst the instruments until he came to a double-edged knife with a wickedly sharp blade. Holding it dagger-wise in his hand he waited until one of the nearer tendrils came sneaking towards him. Bethinking himself, he unstoppered a plastic phial and put it nearby—then he made one clean, slashing cut at the substance, severing the foremost section from the main mass.

It bent and twisted like gelatine over heat. A whisk of the blade and the stuff dropped in the phial. The lid snapped on. For a while the stuff squirmed and slithered on the glass and then became quiescent, gradually turning deep grey in colour and looking no more interesting than a pebble.

"Dies with extreme rapidity," Linida reflected, "but apparently we can't kill it in its entirety without destroying the root—which is presumably somewhere in the strong room. Might use our biggest atom bombs on it later on. For the moment we must get out of here and warn the Highest."

Cal nodded and fled with him from the laboratory. As they went, they informed the immediate staff of the danger, ordered them to move all possible equipment immediately, and then evacuate themselves.

Next, Cal and Linida found themselves being granted an audience with the Highest, and he listened in growing amazement to their story.

"But what is this substance?" he demanded finally. "Cal, have you no conception?"

"None, sir. I withdrew a purplish gas, partly hydrogen, from Sirius—and from the Companion I withdrew a grey gas, which has no parallel in our tables. I sealed them both in the vault side by side and this morning I found the place overflowing with this plasma."

"Did you say you put them side by side?" Linida demanded suddenly, his fierce eyes swinging on Cal.

"Yes, but they were sealed in transmission-booths, radiation proof and...."

"Proof against the radiations we know," the mathematician corrected. "An alien radiation might find the case no more hindrance than plain glass. I have a theory, Highest," he continued, looking at the ruler, "but I must have time to work it out. Whilst I am doing so every effort must be made to stop this substance progressing. I suggest it be atom-bombed and the populace warned to evacuate before it. I don't know what effect it has on living tissue such as ours, but I imagine it will be injurious."

"I will take every necessary step immediately," Cafna Brodix promised, rising majestically.

Linida hesitated no longer. The phial still in his hand, protected by a length of proofed sheeting, he strode actively cut of the sanctum and then down the corridors of the huge administrative building, Cal at his side. So he finally reached his private laboratory. He was looking grimmer than usual as he put the phial down on the bench and drew on flesh-fitting, proofed gloves.

"This stuff weighs heavy," he commented. "Took me all my time to carry this tiny lump in one hand.... You should have taken my advice, son. I warned you what you might get dabbling with alien substances— though I never expected anything like this."

"The Highest gave an order and I tried to obey it," Cal responded unhappily. "In one respect I trust he is satisfied. He wanted something unusual to attract our attention, and he s certainly got it!"

The mathematician said nothing. For a while he stood pondering, his craggy old face lighted by the fitful sunlight through the high window. For all his apparent unshaken calm there was a harassed look about him that Cal was quick to notice—and his spirits sank still lower. If the hard-bitten Kio Linida was becoming alarmed, then there must be danger ahead indeed.

Finally he seemed to make up his mind. Unstoppering the phial, he tipped out the grey, dead-looking substance on to an immaculate gold plate and stood watching it. It remained motionless, evidently quite extinct. Linida prodded it experimentally with a platinum-tipped needle, but no life was apparent. Finally he moved the entire plate to the powerful binocular microscope, screwed in the strongest lens, and peered through it. For a long time Cal was forced to watch that mane of hair drooping over the tubes and the broad shoulders motionless.

"Definitely cellular," the mathematician pronounced

finally. "Or rather multi-cellular. It is of the order of the oldest stuff in the universe—protoplasm, but of a different type from any protoplasm we ever encountered. Therein lies the difficulty!"

His eyes rose from the lens, rapier-keen as he concentrated.

"Even protoplasm has to have something to start it living," Cal pointed out. "I got a *gas*, sir, not a protoplasm."

The mathematician gave a grim smile. "I think, Cal, that what you really got—all unknowingly of course—was a catalyst. Let's go back a little. You say you obtained a gas from Sirius that was mainly hydrogen. *Mainly!* What else was there? What was the hydrogen proportion?"

"Around seventy-five per cent."

"Leaving twenty-five per cent of what?"

"That I don't know," Cal confessed. "I was too busy then to attempt a detailed analysis. There might have been some very rare gases. Certainly there was *one* I couldn't analyze: quite possibly there were others."

"Gases in the free state give off radiation of sorts," Linida mused. "In fact, everything which has molecular activity does. Though we can't prove it with this unfortunate business so far advanced, I think the answer is that the unknown gas percentage in the Sirius sample acted as a radiant catalyst upon the grey gas from the Companion. The booths were not proof against it, and, one affecting the other, this was the outcome—a kind of protoplasm was created."

Cal frowned. "I cannot quite see how, sir."

"Surely you are scientist enough to know that most protoplasmic forms exist in a gaseons state to begin with? Let us go back to the dawn of any planet, which is now populated by living beings. First, the chaotic gases; second, the condensation of the gases into solids; and finally, the activation of solids, by chemical processes, into life. We know that at times there appears a catalyst, which we can only define as an unexplained 'something' reacting upon something else in such a way as to change its nature. Catalysts will always be scientific mysteries."

"Then you mean that the gas from Sirius excited the gas from the Companion to such an extent that it lost its gaseous property and took on life of sorts after expanding outwards from the booth?"

"As lowly protoplasm." Linida was nodding vigorously. "But being of an order we have never yet encountered, it is not destroyed by any method known to us. Remember that you took your samples from suns—gaseous bodies—not planets. Therein lies the difference. The answer is plain: there is something in the makeup of Sirius that brings life to the gas of the Companion. In the same way the makeup of the sun of this system we now occupy excited life in the gases of Earth. It's the old order repeating itself—but this time we face something from an alien quarter of the universe about which we know next to nothing."

Cal was silent, baffled, staring at the grey, inert substance on the bench. Then he looked up sharply and through the window as there came a sudden over-whelming concussion. In the distance fast planes were speeding through the morning heavens over a towering mushroom of smoke.

"Atom bombs," Linida commented dryly. "Of little avail, I am afraid. We should never have dabbled with other parts of the universe—at least not in this fashion. There is no greater error than to bring an alien life away from its surroundings."

"Look, sir!" Cal exclaimed abruptly, pointing. "That can't be the protoplasm, surely? It *couldn't* advance at such a speed, could it?"

The mathematician gazed intently through the window, his eyes narrowed under his tufted brows. From this fairly dominant position in the administrative building it was possible to see most of the massive town. In the further distances, perhaps two miles away, to the left of the smoking ruin that had been the laboratory where Cal had worked, there was moving a brownish carpet with a grey centre. And moving at almost unbelievable speed, swarming up the buildings, flowing along the streets, heading out towards the valley sides where, high up, stood the gargantuan trees of the primeval forest.

"Yes, it's the protoplasm," Linida confirmed at length, his voice grim. "It's obvious what has happened. Bombing the stuff was the last thing we should have done! It exploded it into a thousand pieces and each piece started to become a separate unit and went on growing. We've multiplied the trouble instead of annihilating it."

"We've got to stop it somehow!" Cal insisted urgently. "If it goes on at this rate it will cover the whole city before we know it. Then what will we do?"

"The most sensible thing we can do at this moment, son, is leave this planet and get out into space immediately," Linida said, clenching his fist. "It is not that I do not think we cannot defeat this menace—I believe we could finally—but we just haven't the time. It grows too rapidly." He came to a decision. "Come with me! We must try and make the Highest see how deadly the danger is."

In a few minutes they had once again reached the ruler's sanctum. He was standing thoughtfully beside the window, gazing out on the flowing alien life and the hurried movement of the people as they gravitated towards the town's centre in an effort to escape the plasma.

"Well, Linida?" the ruler asked, turning. "What have you to report? I did what I could to have the stuff destroyed, but apparently without effect."

"Because each section grows," the mathematician explained. "Fission division—the sexual activity of the lowest form of life. My advice, Highest, is to leave this world at the earliest possible moment."

Cafna Brodix gazed in astonishment. "You're not serious, Linida? You cannot be! We, the mightiest scientist, running away from the lowest form of life? It is too absurd!"

"It is common sense!" Linida declared fiercely.

"Though we know most things about science, we need time in which to act, and we just haven't got it. At its present speed this substance will have covered our whole city, inside and out, within a week."

"All the more reason why we should defeat it," the ruler answered in cold pride. "We are an intelligent race who have mastered space and its dimensions. I refuse to allow us to run away like—like amateurs before this alien life. It can be destroyed, and it must be!"

"This is obstinacy, Highest!" Linida protested, glaring. "And it is suicide! A remedy cannot be found in time"

"Perhaps....," Cal started to say, thinking; then he stopped and frowned. The ruler and mathematician looked at him sharply.

"Perhaps what?" Linida snapped.

"I was wondering," Cal resumed. "Cellular life is the basis of this plasma, of course. The right agent to destroy it is yet another cellular life of opposing qualities."

"You mean the basic law of the universe?" the mathematician asked. "That one form of life always devours the other until the finest is left and the residue tamed?"

"Just that," Cal agreed. "We know that the oceans of the world would be choked with life were it not for other life inimical to it which keeps things at a normal level—the Law of Natural Selection. What we have to find is a form of life deadly to this plasma which will attack it."

"Which sounds to me like exchanging one life-menace for another," Linida said curtly.

"That would only happen if this opposing life were uncontrollable," Cal pointed out. "I'm proposing a form of life, under our mastery which, once it has done its work, can be wiped out. That should present no problem since we'll know its makeup."

"I think," the Highest said, "it would be advisable if you made yourself clearer, Cal."

Cal nodded. "I am thinking of the many times we have produced synthetic life in the laboratory, sir. We have made amalgams of all the ingredients that go to make up a living embryo, and have excited life into them by cosmic radiation. That is more or less a routine job. We *could* make synthetic living beings like ourselves at this very moment, as you know, but the law forbids it, 'because it would upset the balance of natural birth'."

"So?" Cafna Brodix questioned.

"Why should we not make microscopic life, after the order of a culture, and instil into it one driving urge—to destroy this plasma and stone life wherever it finds it? That we could do. In the microscopic brain of the culture—nevertheless devised so that it also has the power of reason and understanding—we could impress our orders electrically. We have done it with synthetic beings to make them slaves of a given command: we could do it with cultures, just as a machine made in a certain way will only do that which it is intended it should do. These cultures, in consuming and destroying this Sirian plasma, would multiply, of course, dividing by fission—but once it had finished its task and anni-hilated the plasma, we could destroy it. It would work for us, not against us."

There was a long silence, then Linida shook his maned head impatiently.

"I suppose it could be done," he growled. "Synthetics are a branch of science we have thoroughly mastered—but it would take too long!"

"I could do it in three days and nights," Cal said. "From one set of cultures, others would multiply."

"I still say...," Linida began, but the Highest cut him short.

"A moment, Linida! If there is any chance at all to beat this alien life, it should be taken. Conquests are not made by running away."

The mathematician was silent, looking fiercely out of the window to where the greyish substance was visibly covering the more distant buildings in an engulfing tide.

"Might I ask, Highest, what was done with the apparatus from my laboratory?" Cal asked. "There was the reflector, and my projector-equipment, the computers...."

"They were dismantled and transferred to the Records Hall," the ruler answered. "At the extreme opposite end of the city. The Hall will make an excel-lent temporary laboratory for you. I have given orders for everything to be reset just as it was in the building we have now destroyed."

"Then I believe I might stand a chance," Cal said. "It

will take the plasma at least a week to travel over the entire city; before then I hope to have matters worked out satisfactorily."

"I will not be a party to suicide!" Linida interrupted angrily. "This planet is finished, and the only sane thing to do is get out and take our peoples and valuables with us."

"I forbid it!" the Highest snapped.

"Then, Highest, I regret I must defy you," the mathematician replied. "I do not intend to throw away my life, or that of my daughter. I will take one of the smaller safety spaceships belonging to the cruiser and depart forthwith—whither I don't know. But I will not stop here!"

Linida did not argue any further. Swinging on his heel he left the sanctum. Cal stood with his brows knitted.

"A new thought struck you, Cal?" Cafna Brodix enquired.

"An unhappy one, sir." Cal gave a rueful smile. "I was going to marry Onia Linida, as you well know. It seems as if her father is going to make that impossible."

"I will do what I can to make Linida obey my orders," the Highest said. "In the meantime you have no time to lose. Proceed with your experiments. Whatever you may need in the way of materials, assistants, or equipment will be provided."

Cal nodded and bowed his way out of the chamber. He could have wished for a more settled state of mind in which to work. The thought of having to part from Onia, perhaps forever, made him wonder if it was worth the effort of trying to save things anyway.

CHAPTER SEVEN

Linida, fully decided in his own mind as to his intentions, did not return immediately to his apartment in the city centre—where, he assumed, Onia would already be, with normal work disrupted. Instead, he walked through the city in the direction of the giant isolated hangar where there was housed the monster space-cruiser which had made the trip from Aldebaran.

The men and women hurrying from the plasma some miles in their rear gave the mathematician glances of wonder as he stalked through their midst, going in the opposite direction. Most of the people knew him by sight: his fierce, warrior-like face was easily recognizable, but none stopped to ask him his intentions or warn him of the danger into which he was heading. Not that he needed warning. He knew perfectly well that the plasma was ahead of him—but even so, it was still some distance from the hangar.

Normally there were guards present outside the enormous building, but the pressure of events had evidently driven them away. Linida looked about him, towards the flowing grey substance swallowing the buildings perhaps a mile away; then he opened the combination-lock on the hangar doors. This was simple enough, since his mathematics had made the locks possible.

Entering the enormous space, he stood surveying the cruiser for a moment, then he turned his attention to small, egg-shaped machines lying like midgets of the original in an orderly line at the far end of the hangar. There were six of them. Selecting the one nearest him, Linida entered it and checked it over—its atomic-power motor, its rocket devices, the water and air conditioning plant, and the storage hold. Provisions would be needed and a variety of clothes to meet any particular climate, together with weapons. Then there would be nothing to stop Onia and him from departing into space. It never entered his head that Onia might not be willing to throw in her lot with him. She was his daughter, and that seemed to him sufficient.

With a nod to himself, he stepped out of the machine and walked back to the hangar door opening. Then he came to a stop. Something was creeping round the edge of the door like a waving tendril, feeling its way and spreading gently inwards. Another followed it; then two more appeared on the opposite side. It only took Linida two seconds to grasp the truth. Moving with relentless speed, the plasma had covered the distance to the hangar and was now spreading over it. If once that opening became blocked....

Linida hurled himself towards it, just as a syrupy extension of the viscid substance lowered from the top of the door's outside. He ran into it helplessly, struggling in a cloying tautening mass, slashing savagely with his fists and sending blobs of the stuff in all directions. Everywhere it dropped it bulged and grew, absorbing fantastic life from its own constitution.

Linida hardly had time to check on his physical reactions as he fought to free himself. He was chiefly aware of an intense revulsion, and at the same time a curious tingling throughout his body as though he were absorbing a mild electric shock. He classed it as the effect of radiation....

Then with a mighty effort he dragged himself free, slapping disgustedly at his robes in which gaping holes had been torn. Stumbling, he got away from the building and then looked back at it in alarm. Enormous though it was, the alien substance was flowing gently over it in a grey tide. In an hour it would be covered, and with it would go all chance of reaching either the space-cruiser or the attendant vessels.

Scowling, Linida turned away and hurried city-wards, his body still tingling oddly from his encounter with the stuff. By the time he had reached his apartment, he had a plan in mind. He closed the door slowly behind him, and as he entered the living room Onia came hurrying towards him from the window.

"Father, then you're still safe!" She embraced him thankfully. "I've been so worried about you. I asked everybody I could think of, including the Highest, where you might be—and nobody seemed to know...." Onia broke off, withdrawing her arms suddenly from about her father's shoulders. "You...you feel electrical!" she said in wonder. "Sort of tingling sensation.... I can still feel it."

Linida was silent, musing to himself. Onia looked at him anxiously. "What has happened?" she demanded. "I can't seem to learn anything except that an alien substance from Sirius has broken loose...."

"From the *Companion* of Sirius," Linida corrected harshly. "Or L-19, as it should be properly called. Cal is responsible for the whole thing...." He added the details in a matter-of-fact tone, concluding, "So the only safe course is to leave this planet as fast as we can. Cal thinks he can make cultures in time to stop the stuff. I think he cannot. So we're leaving."

"And going where?" Onia asked in surprise.

"Anywhere away from here. Into space...." Linida walked over to the window, rubbing his faintly tingly arms gently as he did so. "I'd planned to use a small space-cruiser, but that can't be done now. This infernal stuff has smothered the hangar, and it nearly smothered me, too! I got caught in it—hence the tingling sensation."

"I'm *still* tingling," Onia said worriedly.

"The plasma has a high radiation content," her father told her. "That produces an electrical reaction on flesh and blood. Nothing harmful as far as I know at present. But as I was saying, we are going away. My own laboratory hasn't yet been touched and I have enough materials there to make a space machine of my own. I'll summon the necessary engineers to do it."

Onia went over to him slowly. "But—this means that you are afraid!" she exclaimed. "I just can't believe it."

"I? Afraid?" Linida looked at her sharply. "Don't be so ridiculous, girl! I happen to have sanity. We've finished our examination of this world, so why should we stay and jeopardise our lives? I don't intend to."

"But in this gaseous plasma, father, we have something which is unique! Our whole science is made up of investigating the unknown. Here we have something really baffling to defeat—and you want to run away!"

The mathematician turned and met the challenge of his daughter's blue eyes.

"It can't be anything else *but* fear!" she insisted. "And it's such a—a revelation to me that I can't credit it! You, so fierce and commanding, looking so much like a warrior, yet at the first sign of real danger you want to run! Why, father, it makes you recessive, and...."

Onia broke off, her hand flying to her cheek as Linida struck her sharply across the face. His eyes bored at her.

"How dare you?" he whispered, his voice quivering. "You are not here to express your immature opinions, Onia, but to do as you are told! I have decided on what we shall do, and we'll do it!"

Onia threw back her head. She could not know that in belonging to a later school of science than her father, her emotional makeup and his were utterly at variance. Where fear was to her practically unknown, it was a very real thing to her parent, having never had the advantage of scientific nervous control, which had been Onia's from birth. They were parent and child, yet because of science as apart as strangers in their views.

"If you wish to run, father, then run!" Onia said coldly. "Since the Highest and Cal are satisfied that with everybody helping they can defeat this plasma, that's good enough for me. I'm not going with you: I prefer to help Cal."

"Onia, you listen to me...!"

Linida strode forward angrily to seize her arm. but she swung away before he could do so. The door of the apartment slammed in his face and left him breathing hard, his lips tight. Slowly he forced down his temper.

"Fool!" he snapped. "Ignorant little fool—like her mother. No understanding...." He reflected and then shrugged. "If she wants it that way, so be it. It can only mean death...."

He rubbed his arms and shoulders vigorously as the tingling that had been troubling him seemed to be developing into something more in the nature of cramp. Annoyed with himself and furious with Onia, he strode into his bedroom and began to strip. Carefully he examined his massive, still immensely powerful body. Outwardly it was in perfect condition: what was happening inside to account for his queer sensations only instruments could show.

So he redressed himself and in a grim mood left the apartment and returned to his laboratory in the administrative building. The staff, still working normally, since there was no danger as yet at this point of the town, glanced at him but asked no questions. When he was at his fiercest it was wisest to remain quiet.

He locked the laboratory door on the inside and strode over to a cabinet with ground-glass screens. Within it were all the necessary X-ray devices for making a photographic and detailed analysis of his body. He stepped into the cabinet, switched on the current, and waited for perhaps three minutes. Then he stepped out again and studied the automatically developed plates and readings, which gave blood pressure, respiration, and every physical reaction.

His brow darkened at what he read. Musing, he turned to the bench and began to figure rapidly. There was a bleak look in his eyes when he had finished.

"At the most, forty-eight hours to live," he muttered. "It is possible death may come even sooner than that— slow petrifying and then a sudden change of metabolic base. There is no other answer...."

He still could not believe his conclusions, so he turned to them again, checking and rechecking. They showed that the gas of the Companion of Sirius, which had mutated into a semi-solid protoplasmic form under the catalytic effect of the neighbouring gas from Sirius itself, had an extremely high radioactive content, which easily penetrated the interstices of living flesh and impregnated the bloodstream. Here the radioactivity produced extraordinary effects.

It created a quick calcification of the bloodstream, a thickening of its constitution, which sooner or later— within forty-eight hours at the most—must mean complete coagulation and the consequent change of the blood to the consistency of limestone. Such a form the protoplasm itself constantly assumed as its cells died. The grey material it left behind, Linida now realised, was in reality a form of stone, cellular petrifaction, and still radioactive despite its death.

The mathematician passed a hand over his forehead as the facts stared at him; then as he thought further he gave a start.

"Onia!" he gasped. "She complained of tingling after embracing me—that means the radioactivity is transferable from one living being to another, as indeed it must be. Whoever she touches must likewise be impregnated from her and...."

Linida stopped, appalled. He could see the endlessness of the deadly chain he had unwittingly started through his contact with the plasma. Suddenly he made up his mind. Onia had got to be warned before it was too late.

But it *was* too late. Linida, his physical system lacking the refinements of development granted to his daughter, Cal, and others of the later generations, had less resistance to the deadly radioactive energy at work within him. He took three strides towards the laboratory door when the catastrophe came upon him.

He froze in mid-stride, immovable, feeling as though he were held in a giant vice, unable to move hand or foot. A sense of unbelievable pressure crushed down on his brain as circulation ceased. Motionless, a greying statue of a man, he crashed over on his back and lay rigid, his mind foundering in the darkness of death.

＊ ＊ ＊ ＊ ＊ ＊ ＊

Onia's first call after leaving her father was upon the Highest. Normally he would never have granted an audience without an appointment—unless there were extreme urgency—but in this instance Onia's position as daughter of the chief mathematician made matters easier. He sat watching her graceful form as she came hurrying towards the desk.

"My apologies, Highest," she said quickly, "but I am seeking Cal. Where can I find him?"

"Your father did not tell you?" the ruler asked in surprise. "Or maybe you have not seen him...."

"Yes, I've seen him." Onia's lips tightened. "I'm afraid we quarrelled. He is determined to flee from this plasmic menace, but I think it better that we stay and fight. So—well, I want to be of use to Cal. After all, I am a laboratory technician and can probably be of service."

Cafna Brodix smiled gravely in his beard. "It is not your laboratory experience which will be of service, my dear, but your presence alone," he said dryly. "Cal was greatly disturbed when he heard your father say that he was leaving this world and taking you with him."

"Cal thinks that?" Onia gave a start. "I must find him at once; he'll not give of his best until I do. Where is he, Highest?"

"A temporary laboratory has been arranged for him in the Hall of Records at the other end of the town. You will find him there, with others."

"Thank you, Highest. Have I your permission to withdraw?"

"In a moment, my dear...." The ruler looked at her steadily. "Tell me, what plans has your father now?"

"He is still determined to flee this planet. He went to the main hangar, intending to use a slave space-flyer, but the plasma buried the place. Indeed, he had quite a fight to get free, I understand. I think his intention now is to make a space-flyer in his own laboratory."

"I see." Cafna Brodix reflected for a moment; then he wrote out and handed across a permit. "There you are, Onia. That will enable you to enter the Hall of Records without hindrance. I am sure you will be able to give Cal all the encouragement he needs in this hour of crisis."

Onia bowed and withdrew as hastily as dignity permitted.

Once outside, she found it necessary to almost fight her way along the crowded streets as she went towards the opposite end of the town. The people, driven before the plasmic tide, had all converged to the—at present—safer regions of the city centre, overwhelming traffic and all normal means of transport. So Onia pushed and shouldered her way, making the journey on foot.

It took her an hour to reach the Hall of Records, its huge doors sealed and guarded so no disturbance could reach the labouring technicians within. Her officially signed card gave her immediate admission and, finally, within the enormous hall which had been converted into a replica of Cal's original laboratory, she came upon him. He and several technicians were working under the glare of shadowless cold-light globes.

"Cal...!" Onia moved swiftly towards him, and he looked up from the experimental bench at which he was working. Immediately his face lighted with joy.

"Onia, it's you!" He caught her in his arms as she reached him, held her tightly to him. For the moment all thought the work upon which he was engaged deserted him. The technicians glanced at each other and continued with their various tasks. Cal looked towards them, then led the girl out of earshot.

"I've seen the Highest," Onia explained quickly, her eyes bright. "He's permitted me to help you in every way possible."

"That's wonderful, of course—but what about your father? I heard him say he...."

"Yes, I know. I disagreed with him.... This is such a wonderful thing you're doing, Cal," Onia went on earnestly. "Trying to destroy this plasma—and I want to help you do it. You *will* destroy it, you know; I'm sure of it."

Cal smiled. "So far we're doing all right, but it's going to be tough work."

"Father said something about your making cultures to destroy the plasma. Is that correct?"

"It is—but there are obstacles to overcome. To fashion the cultures is simple, but to breathe life into them may present difficulties. They are specially constructed with quite a little of Sirius' qualities in their makeup. That very chemical fact may render it difficult to make them live.... Not like straightforward synthesis, which responds to cosmic radiation. However, we'll cross that bridge when we come to it...."

Cal stopped talking, puzzling something over to himself, then to Onia's surprise he put out his hand and clasped her arms.

"Then I wasn't mistaken," he said, mystified. "You are *tingling*! When I took hold of you a moment ago—and again now—I detected a mild shock, almost an electric current."

Cal lowered his hand and looked at her. Though he was no longer in contact with her, he could still feel an inexplicable quivering and tautening of nerves and muscles.

"That's father's fault," Onia explained. "I've been tingling ever since I embraced him when I greeted him. I'm getting used to it now, though. It'll wear off."

Cal's expression changed. "Just a minute, Onia. I want to know more about this. How do you mean—your father's fault? What did he do?"

"Got mixed up with the plasma...." Onia gave the details and Cal listened with a troubled frown. He seemed about to say something, then one of the technicians called him. He hurried over to the testing bench, the girl following behind to watch the proceedings.

"Seems to be about complete, Cal," one of the men said, motioning.

For a moment there was silence in the immense converted hall.

In a large sealed, transparent globe—upon which

there had up to this moment been trained a battery of electronic-patterning beams—a minute pinhead object floated in pellucid fluid. It appeared as little more than a drifting speck of dust, until Cal switched on an instrument. Immediately the globe became bathed in blinding light, and its contents were reflected into a projection-machine.

Upon a nearby screen, twelve feet by six, there appeared an image of the thing in the globe. Now, as the scientists studied it, it could be seen as perfectly formed with a head, mandibles, six legs, and claw appendages.

"Is that the culture?" Onia asked, staring at the screen fixedly.

"That's it," Cal agreed. "Magnified some ten thousand times. It is made of synthetic material, and was created by patterning the material with electronic beams—the equivalent of a knife, only infinitely more accurate. Nor is this culture, or the ones which will follow it from the original pattern, by any means unintelligent...."

Cal switched off the apparatus and looked first at the girl and then the technicians.

"I'd better explain," he said. "This culture has a brain, but at the moment it is so much dead tissue, no more alive than is the rest of the culture's body. You might call it an atom-sized brain, in that it packs the essence of impressions, instead of having them in a diffused form, as do we human beings. Once it comes to life, it will be capable of grasping and understanding that which is going on around it.

"However, those details are not important. On its brain—and the brains of the cultures yet to be made—we shall electronically impress one command. It will be— 'Consume the stone and plasma life wherever you find it'! That, of course, is how it sounds in plain words: actually it will be expressed in vibrations. In other words, the basic urge of this creature when it comes to life will be to destroy the plasma and stone. Understand?"

The technicians nodded. Onia asked a question.

"Do you mean it consumes the stone and plasma for nourishment, and that if it doesn't, it will die? Which gives it a vital reason for destroying the stone and plasma."

"That's it exactly," Cal agreed. "It is so constituted that it must consume the Sirian stuff—in order to live. We are simply duplicating the ancient order of the universe—kill or be killed. Altogether there will be five hundred of these cultures which, when they are infused with life, will be turned loose to attack the plasma. As they evolve, they will procreate by fission, as do all cultures. In an hour there will be ten thousand cultures. In twenty-four hours there will be two hundred and forty thousand cultures—and so on. An ever-growing army to wipe out the Sirian plasma until finally it is consumed right back to its roots. When that is accomplished, all we have to do is destroy the cultures—a simple enough job by supersonic vibrations. Thus-wise I believe we can win our fight."

"And will the cultures which are spawned have the same basic destructive urge as the parents?" Onia enquired.

"Certainly—just as the instinct of a new-born infant is to eat. The basic urge is handed on independent of everything else. I'm sure," Cal finished, "that we have a mighty weapon. As I have mentioned, the only trouble with this culture and those to come is that they are different in constitution to anything we have made before. To instil into them the urge to destroy the plasma would be useless without making them capable of doing it—so in digestive and other details we have had to include new synthetic patterns, which may prove difficult when we come to infuse life into them. That we'll know later. For the moment our task is to create the remaining cultures—then we'll what can be done to make them live."

"But surely," Onia said, "if you bring life into this single one and turn it loose, it will itself create an army in no time?"

"True—but five hundred of them will make an army so much bigger when you consider the multiplication of one by five hundred. For the sake of some twelve hours, it is better to make an army really capable of fighting the plasma than just turning one culture loose, which, of itself, would never be able to procreate fast enough to cope with the situation. So—" Cal turned actively to the instruments—"to work!"

CHAPTER EIGHT

In the meantime Cafna Brodix had not been idle. Realizing the nature of the crisis on his hands, but thoroughly convinced that Cal could cope with it, it lay with him to calm the fears of the city's inhabitants being driven before the inexorably advancing plasma.

Before deputations could reach him, demanding to know why the planet could not be evacuated, he gave a tele-radio speech, seen and heard from the public viewing screens in all parts of the city and public buildings. In it he managed to instil an air of complete calmness, the keynote being that as scientists they had never yet run away from a problem but had always mastered it—as they would this time. Indeed they had to, for the space-cruiser and attendant machines were smothered in the alien life, and there was not the time to build another cruiser.

It was now a case of stand and conquer—or perish. That this was a battle which science, for once, might lose was something Cafna Brodix did not mention, even if it occurred to him. His trust in Cal's ingenuity and high purpose remained unshaken. His final words held out a promise that once the plasma was defeated the race, far more knowledgeable for its experience, would travel to far distant Sirius and his Companion to examine it at close quarters, since here there existed an amazing form of life that must make any planets of the Sirian system worthy of study.

To a great extent these assurances calmed the populace, but the Highest did not trust entirely to this. He deployed guards at strategic points to keep order until the danger was over. He had scouts to watch and report on the progress of the plasma and its general direction. It seemed to be still moving at the same relentless pace, but the fact that it swarmed inside the giant buildings as well as over them caused its actual advance to slow up as it oozed into every niche and cranny. At a reasonable estimate it seemed that the further reaches of the city, where lay Cal's temporary laboratory and the administrative buildings, would be safe for another two or three days.

These major details taken care of, the Highest turned his attention to another more personal matter. It seemed obvious to him, from what Onia had said, that Kio Linida was still determined to defy orders, and if the populace saw that one man had succeeded in building a space machine in order to escape, there would be unpredictable consequences. All attempts at maintaining law would collapse. Linida had to be stopped—and to this end the Highest issued his orders, summoning the captain of the Guard for his instructions.

"You will not treat Linida as a common offender

against the law, Captain," the ruler explained, as the guardsman stood at his desk. "He holds a high position in our community; but you will stop him from building a space machine in his laboratory which, I understand from his daughter, is his intention. He is deliberately flouting my orders and that, with all the respect I have for his ability, I cannot permit. You will place your men in his laboratory and keep a watch on his movements—nothing more. He is at liberty to work normally, but not on a space machine. You understand?"

"Perfectly, Highest," the Captain assented.

"Very well; that is all. Report back to me as to procedure. You will probably find Linida in his laboratory in this administrative building; if not, then at his city apartment, which should be still untouched by the plasma's advance."

The Captain saluted and went on his way. In five minutes he was knocking on the inner door of the mathematician's laboratory, having been informed by the staff that their chief was at work in there. A long silence followed the knocking and the guardsman looked questioningly at his five subordinates.

"Go and see if anybody has a key," he ordered finally. "It does not seem possible that Linida could have left without being seen."

One of the men departed to obey the order, but he returned empty-handed.

"Linida is the only one with a key, sir," he announced. "I also checked up on whether he might have left.

Apparently he has not."

The Captain again knocked heavily on the door; then, as he still received no answer, he stood back a little and turned his proton-gun on the lock. It dissolved in an evanescent flaring of intense white flame. A single kick sent the door swinging inwards on its hinges.

The guards entered the area and looked about them, to pause as they beheld the motionless figure on the floor, curiously rigid and grey. Instantly the Captain hurried forward. The moment he touched the fallen figure he withdrew his hand sharply and shook it.

"He feels electrical!" he said in wonder.

The guards looked at each other: then despite the uncomfortable sensation it gave them they heaved the body upright, looking into the dead grey face and wide open eyes.

"It *is* Linida," the Captain muttered, astounded. "But what has happened to him? He looks more like a statue than a man— Why does he give off such a strong electrical emanation, I wonder?"

These were problems that he was not competent to solve. He motioned to his subordinates and between them they dragged the immensely heavy corpse to a low-built couch against the wall, laying the dead mathematician upon it.

"We must inform the Highest immediately," the Captain said at last, rubbing his tingling hands together. "This is beyond our understanding. Maybe he was engaged upon some kind of experiment which petrified him."

He cast a final, bewildered look about the scene, then with his men accompanying him he left, giving orders to the staff on his way from the building that nothing in the laboratory was to be touched.

In half an hour he had returned, the staff coming to respectful attention as they realized the Highest himself was in their midst. He passed them by with a venerable smile, his flowing robes rustling softly, and went on his way to the mathematician's quarters. Here he looked for a time at the body, touched it, then recoiled swiftly as he too, felt the strange, twisting thrill which shot through his nerves and muscles.

"Extraordinary," he commented, stroking his beard. "I quite fail to understand it. It would seem as though Linida has turned into stone. I wonder now...." His eyes narrowed. "His daughter did tell me that he had had a fight with the plasma. Could it by any chance have affected him in this way? If so...."

He became silent, the quality of his thoughts startling him considerably. His own body was curiously stiff and tingling. He, as Linida had been, was of the earlier school whose physical resistance had not the power to combat for any protracted length of time the deadly radioactive processes transmitted by the dead plasma, into which Linida had been converted.... Much of the radioactive power still remained, and could only become dormant with the passage of time. Even in death the mathematician had handed on his malady.

"I will contact Cal Vandos at the laboratory," the Highest said at length, turning. "He may be able to give an explanation for the trouble. Do you men still feel ill-effects from handling this corpse?"

They nodded with obvious uneasiness. The Captain answered for them.

"A feeling of cramp, Highest, which so far hasn't shown any sign of wearing off."

"Quite so. Electrical, I imagine. Let me give you a word of warning, Take care to avoid contact with people—at least for the time being. Apparently this body is emanating some kind of energy, the exact nature of which I do not know, but it is plain that it can be transmitted from one person to another. For the moment you may go, and you are relieved from duty to prevent you mixing with other people. I will summon you when I have further information."

The men saluted and marched out with military precision. For a long time the Highest stood frowning and thinking; then he wandered across to the testing bench and glanced about it in the hope that h might afford some clue to explain the mathematician's strange death. It was not long before his gaze fell upon the scratch pad covered in calculations.

The Highest raised the pad and studied it; then he slowly settled down on the stool and pondered the meaning of the figures. It was not long before he understood them, and the fate that had overtaken Linida, and which must finally overtake him—sooner than those of younger consideration.

An hour passed. He still read the notes and brooded. Two hours passed and the laboratory staff began to wonder why the Highest was so long in leaving, until finally one of them plucked up enough courage to go and investigate.

When he cautiously entered the laboratory and looked about him, he saw a motionless grey figure seated at the test bench, the notebook in his hand, his magnificent visage frozen into utter immovability amidst the flowing white of his beard and hair.

The technician fled, his voice echoing down the corridor as he went—

"Quickly, quickly! All of you! The Highest is dead! Turned to stone...!"

* * * * * * *

Of these events, as he laboured with his fellow scientists—Onia helping wherever she could—Cal had no knowledge; but the news of the strange death of the Highest could not possibly escape being broadcast by the general radio speakers.

It was as he controlled the electrical device, which was patterning cultures after the design of the first one, that Cal heard the facts. So did Onia. So did the technicians. At first they were disinterested; then they paused in their work to listen to the amazing announcement, presumably being made by the second-in-authority to Cafna Brodix and one of the city's ruling Council.

"What has caused the mysterious petrifying of the Highest and First Mathematician, Kio Linida, is at present unknown, but a Captain of the Guard, who was present with the Highest when the stony body of Kio

Linida was found, has said that the Highest made some reference to the plasma which is attacking our city. It would appear from this that Linida came into contact with the plasma, and that may have been the predisposing cause of his strange death, a condition which he unknowingly handed on to...."

Cal reached out and snapped off the radio. He glanced at the technicians.

"Carry on without me for a while," he said. "I have something I wish to check...."

Since it was not their business to ask questions they obeyed.

Cal took Onia's arm and led her away from the testing bench until they reached a private ante-room off the main hall which had been assigned to Cal as his temporary living quarters.

"Onia," he said quietly, "that message brings up something which has got to be faced. I don't like asking a lot of questions right on top of your hearing of your father's death, but I really...."

"I know just what you are going to ask, Cal," Onia interrupted. "About this malady—or whatever it is."

"Yes. You said that when you embraced your father when he returned from his fight with the plasma at the space ship hangar he was tingling—and that you tingled thereafter. Do you still feel that sensation?"

Onia nodded slowly. "Yes—only it is more of a numbness now. A kind of heaviness. I don't think I ever felt like it before. And for the first time in my life I have a headache."

"My own symptoms exactly, only I thought it might be from overwork on this culture business.... The only answer is that we are both impregnated with something. I don't know what, and I haven't the instruments here to make an examination—but if the fate of your father and the Highest is any indication, the future doesn't look too bright."

The girl's blue eyes were unflinching.

"You mean we might die, as they did, by turning to stone?"

"The possibility is there, Onia—but not everybody in the city will turn to stone, surely? Only those who...." Cal stopped, frowning worriedly. "Tell me—on your way here did you come in contact with anybody?"

"Many people. I could hardly do anything else with the city so crowded...." Onia's expression changed abruptly and her hand went to her mouth in alarm. "Great heavens, you don't mean that I may have handed it on?"

"It looks that way, since your father handed it to you and you to me—and so on. Those whom you touched or brushed against as you came here were doubtless impregnated too; they will touch others. There is no way of seeing the end of it! Which seems to suggest a radioactive power of some kind," Cal finished, the scientist in him dominating again for a moment. "That would also account for the vaguely electrical sensation."

"Then what do we do?" Onia asked. "Where is the use in going on in the effort to destroy the plasma if we are doomed anyway?"

"We must go on because some may survive," Cal answered quietly. "It is for those few that we have to work. There is also the chance that this malady which has affected you and me may have an antidote which, given the time, I might find. It all depends on how rapidly it affects us. Yes, we must go on," he insisted. "Those technicians who are helping me in the lab have not as yet been in physical contact with either you or me. They can remain free if we avoid touching them. Take care not to say anything to them, or else their very fear of touching us may make their work clumsy and ruin the job on which we're engaged. Now, we'd better get back and help them."

Onia nodded, still unable to assimilate the stunning fact that she and Cal were probably doomed to early and fantastic extinction through an agency they did not even understand. How true her father's words had been—that it was dangerous to dabble in alien substances from other worlds—Onia was only just commencing to realize...too late.

She was moodily silent as the creation of the remaining cultures progressed. Cal for his part was too absorbed in his work to pass anything but scientific comments. He was watching the arrival of cultures in the giant globe as the electronic patterners constantly moulded them out of almost invisible synthetic material swimming in jelly from in the globe's fluid.

Though Onia made no word of complaint, she could feel the queer symptoms, which had begun with tingling gradually becoming less easy to bear. Her limbs felt incredibly heavy, so much so that she took to sitting down in between the intervals of lending assistance. Her head, too, was throbbing violently as though some inner pressure were trying to explode it. Cal, too, felt the same symptoms, but to a great extent his absorption in his work prevented him from concentrating too much upon them. It was only when he relaxed for the rest period that he realized how ill he really felt.

"Call me if anything happens," he instructed the chief technician. "When the last culture is made, I mean. After that we have only to bring them to life. Prepare the cosmic radiation equipment in readiness."

The technician nodded—then he reached forward suddenly to catch Onia's arm as, in getting to her feet, she reeled giddily. Instantly he snatched his hand back, perplexed, and the girl stared at him through dull blue eyes.

"You—you touched me!" she whispered.

The technician rubbed his tingling fingers. "My apologies, Onia," he said respectfully. "I feared you were going to fall. You look unwell...."

"You touched me!" Onia repeated hoarsely. "You shouldn't have done it...."

Cal stopped her by taking her gently in his arms. He glanced at the puzzled scientist.

"I'm afraid she is unwell," Cal explained. "Thanks for your assistance, Laj. Call me when I'm needed."

Before she could say anything more, Onia found herself half carried away across the hall. When they had reached the anteroom, Cal set her down gently on the couch.

"I don't think you said enough to frighten him, dearest," he murmured, pushing the fair hair back from her forehead.

"But, Cal, you should have let me warn him that...."

"It wouldn't have done any good. We're at the crucial stage of the experiment now with the cultures nearly completed. If he gets afraid and walks out, so will the others, and I can't finish the job without them. Inevitably, he will touch the other technicians. Inevitably, I am afraid, we shall all die. But if we succeed in liberating the cultures and destroying the plasma and stone life, we shall at least have accomplished something for those who may still remain."

Onia was silent, stirring her leaden limbs. Cal put a hand to his throbbing eyes.

"I'll get some food," he said, "and some sandwiches. This may make us feel better."

He was absent some time and returned to find Onia half asleep. He aroused her sufficiently to make her drink some powerful restorative essence, and the effect was little short of magical. In the space of a few minutes the languor vanished from her bearing and the heaviness dropped from her limbs. She even smiled with something of her former gaiety.

"That's better!" she exclaimed, sitting up. "I do believe I'm going to be all right."

Cal gave her a serious smile and drank some of the essence himself; then he sat considering his physical reactions. The sensation of well-being which gradually flowed through him did not deceive him in the least, any more than did the cessation of his headache. As a scientist he had already arrived at the conclusion that the radioactive effect was impregnating the blood-stream, causing it to clog and thereby producing heaviness of the limbs and pressure within the head. The essence counteracted the effect—but only for a time. He sat brooding over that which was to come. When the essence had spent itself, the deadening coagulation would set in again.

"What is the matter?" Onia asked, rising and then seating herself at the table beside him. "Are you not glad to feel better?"

"Of course—but I'm tired. I've been working hard." He looked at her steadily. "Don't put too much store on this sudden relief, Onia. It may only be temporary."

"If it is we can keep this way by drinking essence."

"Maybe—but there'd have to be a reckoning some-time...."

Cal broke off and turned as one of the technicians came hurrying in. It was plain that only extreme urgency could have made him burst into private quarters in this fashion.

"What is it, Laj?" Cal looked at him sharply.

"The plasma! It has reached here— You'd better come."

Cal stared. "But it can't have! It had a whole city to traverse. It couldn't have got here for two days...."

"Apparently it is a stray tributary of the stuff, sir,

which has flowed round the back of the city—as far as we can judge from the windows."

Cal did not hesitate a second longer. With Onia behind him, he raced into the giant hall and then looked towards the main doorway, which led out into the street. Plasma was oozing under it and creeping along the polished metal floor. Presumably the guards outside had seen the stuff coming and run for their lives without giving warning.

"Quickly!" Cal snapped. "Drop the safety shutter over the inside of the door. You, Tilan, get the proton-beam projector ready."

Both technicians obeyed instantly. The movement of a switch released a massive two-inch thick metal door from its slots which crashed down on the inside of the doors themselves. Normally it was used when the Hall of Records closed for the night as a protection against any possible climatic upheaval—by no means unusual on this young world. In this instance it had a better purpose. As it fell, severed sections of the plasma flew in all directions, and each section grew and swelled.

Cal swung to the protonic-gun and sighted it. When he pressed the button its deadly emanations caused the plasma to disintegrate but it did not kill it. Each dissociated piece grew swiftly into a new form and spread, blindly investigative.

"No use," Cal said, switching off. "Nothing kills this stuff except to choke it off for lack of air—an impossibility with the whole mass. Get those containers," he instructed, and nodded to four giant bins with hermetically sealed lids.

The lids were quickly stripped off, then in the lead and with the technicians behind him he moved to where the small plasma mounds were growing steadily.

A scooping movement of the bins' thin edges along the floor was sufficient to sweep the deadly stuff from its hold. The lids were clamped back and quickly resealed with one of the many instruments. A long pause followed, then Cal shook one of the bins gently up and down and was rewarded by a rattling sound as though a stone were within.

"That's done it!" he exclaimed thankfully. "It has died and changed to its dead-cell substance. If only we could asphyxiate and muzzle all of it in this fashion!"

Wishful thinking having no place in his makeup, he turned to the high windows, climbed up on the bench, and looked outside. Onia and the technicians presently climbed up beside him. They were faced by a none too cheerful prospect. As Laj had said, a single arm of the stuff had flowed round the rear of the city from the distant smothered hangars and, having absorbed one or two nearby buildings, was now crawling and flowing relentlessly over this Hall of Records. It spread into the distance as a grey, viscid sea under the dim light of the sunset.

In the city centre the way was clear, but at its furthest extremity the grey barrier reared, moving onwards steadily, presumably filling all buildings as well as covering them. Of the populace there was little sign, the explanation probably being that most of them had fled to the surrounding jungle to escape the terror—only perhaps to die in a different way from the rigours of a young world, amongst hardships to which they were totally unaccustomed.

"The plasma won't get in here," Cal said finally. "These windows are solidly built into their frames and the only opening was the door. Better close the vents," he added. "We can use the air-conditioning apparatus."

Two of the technicians jumped down and closed the switch that sealed the vents. The building now, for all practical purposes, was airtight. For a long time the group watched the mass sliding over the windows and blotting out the deep twilight, until at last every window was blacked out with a greyish curtain which slowly changed to the hard consistency of stone.

"Apparently," Cal said, when they had all returned to the floor of the hall, "we are buried in here—though we can keep in touch with the outer world by radio if we need. Nothing for it but to continue with our work. How far have you got, Laj?"

"Just when the plasma arrived, we had created the five hundredth culture," he responded, and pressed finger and thumb into his eyes. "I—I will continue as you order, sir, whilst you and Onia rest."

"We've had some essence and are in no need of rest," Cal told him. "But you are—and you too, Tilan. I'll call you when I need you."

Wearily the two technicians wandered off into the anteroom, dragging their legs as though they were too much weight for them. Cal shot the girl a significant look. He noticed that her eyes were looking drowsy again and, from his own slowly returning symptoms, judged that the effect of the essence was wearing off. With an effort he fought against the sense of crushing pressure in his skull, and looked at the big container where swam the microscopic mist of five hundred cultures.

"Then we are ready for the electronic brain impressions?" Cal questioned of the two men still left—and they nodded.

Apparently, so far, they had escaped any contact with the technicians who had gone off duty. They looked weary, but bore no signs of the marked illness now so visible in the grey complexions of Cal and Onia.

"We can do it, Cal, if you and Onia wish to rest," one of them volunteered. "You both look worn out...."

"This is no time to think of ourselves," Cal said, with an effort. "Thank you, though, for your consideration. Set up the micro-impressor," he ordered. "You, Flenj, remove the culture-globe to the transmission chamber."

The man known as Flenj lifted the globe carefully and placed it within a four-walled metal container immediately under an instrument resembling a complicated photographic enlarger. Cal, his nerves acting, switched on the impressor's power, and under the influence of the mysterious current disturbing it, the fluid in the globe containing the cultures swirled and eddied silently.

"None of you make a sound whilst I concentrate,"

Cal ordered, slipping a cap of bristling electrodes over his head and then buckling it beneath his chin. "I must make no mistake with this mental order...."

Onia sat down heavily and remained motionless, watching. The technicians remained standing, not even the sound of their breathing escaping them. Cal closed his eyes for a moment or two, his whole expression one of profound mental effort; then he relaxed and moved the helmet from his skull. Reaching out, he switched off the impressor.

"So far all is in order," he proclaimed. "Since the brain of each one of these cultures is identical in pattern, and the only part of the organism able to receive and retain a mental impression, it is obvious that that highly concentrated, amplified mental command of mine must have been equally impressed on each of the five hundred. Each one henceforth has only one basic urge—to destroy the plasma and stone life, to consume it for its own nourishment. Whatever other impressions the cultures may store, we cannot predict. The task now is to bring them to life. Flenj, did Laj set up the cosmic-radiation machine as I ordered?"

"Yes, Cal—everything is ready." The technician motioned to the massive instrument, designed after the fashion of an X-Ray projector, but emitting the ultra-short wavelength of pure cosmic rays.

Cal sat down heavily. He had not intended doing so. He just could not help himself. Suddenly his legs seemed unable to support him and he thudded down and there remained, bemused. He rubbed his forehead impatiently, the two technicians looking at him in surprise.

"Cal, you really *should* rest!" Onia insisted, still seated nearby. "I should too. We both need it...."

"Rest!" Cal gestured impatiently. "What time is there for that?"

With a tremendous effort he got on his feet and went across to the bench, checking over the cosmic radiation projector. His examination complete he gave a nod.

"Put the culture-globe on the focussing-plate, he ordered.

This was duly done, Flenj setting the globe carefully on the circular grid immediately in line with the projector's blunt snout. Cal closed the switch and the apparatus hummed gently. There was no sign of any radiation coming forth from it. The only visible evidence of the ultra-short wavelength exactly duplicating the cosmic radiation of free space was the violent agitation of the fluid within the globe.

Cal stood watching it intently, his face gaunt in the shadowless glare. Onia forced herself to her feet and went over to him, her tired eyes staring at the mist in the globe. The silence was broken for a moment by a slithering as of melting snow on the roof. Evidently a sizeable portion of plasma had slipped transiently from its hold.

"This is taking much longer than it should," Cal said at length, frowning. "Normally it takes only two minutes to infuse life into synthetic tissue...."

"Probably the new ingredients we had to use," Flenj

pointed out, and Cal gave a grim nod.

"Yes, I was afraid this might happen...." He checked the readings and then said in a puzzled voice: "They're partly alive—but nothing more. Their brains are storing impressions, but their remaining physical structure refuses to react."

He stood pondering this, fingering his aching forehead.

"Evidently, cosmic radiation isn't the right answer this time," he said at last. "It works on the brains only, which won't do at all.... Here we are, within an ace of victory, and can't bring the infernal stuff fully to life! What else is there outside cosmic radiation?"

To this profound problem nobody had an immediate answer—until Onia suddenly seemed to recall something.

"I remember something father once said," she mused, and Cal turned to her eagerly. Whatever else her father might have been, his scientific skill had always been beyond question.

"He didn't believe that cosmic rays are the basic exciting cause of all forms of life," she explained. "I can hardly remember his theories because he was always so complicated in the way he expressed them. His conception was that cosmic radiation excites life only in certain cases—such as in the brains of these cultures, perhaps—but other chemical aggregates might require a different excitation.... For instance, he had volumes of notes on the causes of life on this planet. His theory was that it was the sun itself that created the life through its seventh-octave radiation. Cosmic radiation had nothing to do with it, according to him. That much I do remember...."

"Then why have we been successful up to now in infusing life into synthetic tissue by cosmic radiation?" Cal asked.

"I suppose it's because the particular tissue you made was sympathetic to that wavelength. Here you have a different form of tissue—except for the brain material—and it won't react, whereas the brain does. Why not try solar power on the remaining portions of these cultures' bodies and see what happens?"

Cal thought it out for a while. "Very well," he agreed finally. "I don't mind what we do just as long as we get some results."

"That means waiting until morning," Flenj pointed out. "At the moment it's about midnight."

"That needn't worry us," Cal told him. "Time's pressing. We'll use the X-ray telescope." He nodded to its giant length nearby. "We'll elevate the centre bar and turn the object lens towards the floor. The light-photon attractor will drive its X-ray beam through the Earth's bulk to where the sun is. We shall get just the same effect as though no solid were intervening."

Flenj nodded, and without waiting to be told he went to work with his two comrades to adjust the giant to the required position, which necessitated the control chair of the instrument being swung into the air on its portable cradle. While the preparations were going ahead to centre the sun, now halfway to the Antipodes,

Cal took a chance to rest. Onia came and sat beside him.

"Do you suppose some more essence would help us?" she asked, and he smiled wearily.

"It probably would for the time being, but the reaction would be worse than our present condition. At least we can still get about, and think—to a certain extent. All I'm interested in doing is making these cultures come fully to life. After that I'll concentrate exclusively on our own troubles and try and find an antidote."

Onia got to her feet. "I'm going to try some essence, anyway, otherwise I'll be too stiff to move at all in a while. I feel as though my hands and feet don't exist anymore."

She turned and walked unsteadily across the hall. Cal gave himself up to brooding, watching the activity with the reflector. When Onia returned again, she was looking less grey and exhausted, an abnormally bright sparkle in her eyes. With her too, the two technicians who had been having their spell of rest. They looked none the better for it. Grey-faced, grimly accusing, they gazed down on Cal

"Something wrong?" he asked listlessly.

"I suspect, Cal, that a good deal is wrong," Laj answered. "Both Tilan and I are ill. We are weighted down in some unexplained fashion, and suffering from spells of numbness. From the behaviour of Onia here, before she drank some essence, I think I'm right in saying that she has the same malady. It would seem it is affecting you, too.... At least we are entitled to know what is wrong."

"Since you can no longer leave this building upon hearing the truth, you may as well have the facts," Cal responded—and gave them. The two technicians listened in silence. The remaining two, working on the reflector, kept their distance.

"Which means that the petrifying death which overtook the Highest and Linida will presently overtake us?" Tilan asked finally.

"Unless time permits of us finding an antidote, yes," Cal agreed quietly. "Has I told you all this before, you might have stopped working. I couldn't afford that risk."

"We are scientists, Cal," Laj said, shrugging. "We would not have deserted the battle. As you have pointed out, we have to go on for the sake of those who may yet live—our two friends over there, for instance," he added, and nodded to the remaining technicians.

Cal struggled to his feet. "I should have known that I could rely on you," he said, and turned to the reflector with the temporarily revived Onia moving behind him.

"Everything is in order," Flenj announced. "The reflector is trained on the sun and following him. To redirect the solar radiations is your job, Cal."

Cal began to mount the narrow cat-ladder, which led up to the control seat at the reflector's summit. Half way up, however, his labouring muscles refused to act. He swayed giddily, clutched helplessly at the ladder rungs, and then slipped. Instantly, Flenj and his companion dashed forward and caught him, cushioning his fall.

He staggered to his feet and gave a troubled smile.

"Thanks," he said in gratitude. "Apparently I'm not up to this sort of work at the moment...."

Suddenly he whipped himself away and the supporting hands fell away from him.

"In saving me you have also come into contact with me," he said, in sudden anxiety. "That was the very thing I wanted to prevent."

Flenj and his fellow scientist rubbed at their tingling fingers.

"Just in the way of things, Cal, I'm afraid," Flenj said at length. "We couldn't let you fall and not try to save you.... In any case we'd probably have touched each other sooner or later; in this confined space in which we're working it could hardly be helped. Shall I go up the ladder?" he asked.

"How did I ever come to think that you fellows might have deserted me?" Cal whispered. "You've given me unswerving loyalty, and even your lives. There's got to be a reward for that. There's *got* to be!" he insisted, with sudden energy. "We'll beat this infernal plasma yet and cure ourselves. Yes, Flenj, get up the ladder," he instructed. "Fit the reflector eyepiece into position and link it to the prismatic tube. In that way we can reverse the solar image and have it pointing downwards instead of up. I'll do the rest."

Flenj began to ascend steadily, and, at the lofty summit of the inverted reflector, followed out his orders. Then he came down to the floor again, and, with the other technicians, helped Cal in setting up the complicated magnetic sifting device by which there was drawn from the sun's image his seventh-octave radiation without his light and heat waves. It was a task which took two hours, but when the thing was done, the instruments showed that through the transformer-transmitter there was passing no solar light—only a steady, unvarying wavelength corresponding to the seventh solar octave.

The culture-globe was removed from the plate of the cosmic ray projector and placed exactly within the range of the radiation; then once again there followed that long, expectant pause. Seconds crept into minutes, but nothing happened. The cultures remained motion-less.

"Useless," Cal whispered, his face haggard. "On this last lap it looks as if we're beaten...." He beat his forehead impatiently. "In the name of cosmos, if only I didn't have to battle with this physical condition, too! I can hardly think straight—hardly move...."

He crept to a nearby chair and sat down leadenly, sinking his head in his hands. Laj and Tilan joined him, little better as far as energy went. Flenj and his comrade, as yet not unduly overcome by their malady, remained beside the culture-globe, contemplating it. Onia, her previous evanescent strength beginning to desert her again, drifted towards the radio equipment and looked at it.

"Any use switching on and seeing what is happening to the rest of the city?" she enquired.

"What does it matter?" Cal asked listlessly. "We

can't get out of here; we're all facing certain extinction—and we've lost our battle. No, Onia—never mind the radio. It's not going to make an atom of difference to us what is happening elsewhere. Everything—all possible interest—is centred right here, and we're like a collection of infernal dummies with not a thought in our heads!"

Nobody commented. Onia drifted away from the radio and presently sat down near the reflector, gazing at it. After a while she turned her head sharply to look at Cal.

"In making these cultures," she said, "you say you included some new ingredients. What were they exactly?"

Cal looked at her drowsily. "I'd take too long to explain."

"I don't mean in detail...." Onia came over to him, her face urgent. "What I am wondering about is the Sirian ingredients you mentioned as having been incorporated in the cultures."

"What about them?"

"Well, why not try radiations from Sirius to try and bring the cultures to life? There seems to be something about Sirius which acts as a catalyst, so why not his radiations? So far you have only used cosmic radiation, which has brought the brains of these cultures to life: Sirian radiation might bring them completely to life."

"That," Cal said, forcing himself to alertness, "is perhaps *it*! Quickly, Flenj; get the reflector turned right way round and focus on Sirius!"

Flenj wasted no time in doing so. Sirius being in the night sky, through the clouds of which the X-ray apparatus easily penetrated, there was no difficulty in locating him. Cal dragged himself to the control chair—now at floor level again—and seated himself heavily, his fingers on the control switches.

Without needing to be told what to do, Flenj, with Laj helping him, fixed in the magnetic-sifter to the reflector's main lens, which meant that the globe of cultures still in line with the sifter was now receiving the radiations of Sinus instead of the sun.

"It may work," Cal breathed, watching the globe fixedly. "Since Sirian gas had a catalytic effect on the Companion gas and brought it to life, his radiations might equally affect the parts of these cultures which are attuned to consume the plasma life."

Onia moved to within a few feet of the reflector and stood watching intently.

"Though it may be the answer, Cal, it's dangerous," she said presently. "With Sirius everything seems to be dangerous!"

"Whether it is or not, Onia, we have to risk it."

"My only fear is that we may bring something worse down upon us," Onia muttered. "Training pure Sirian radiation into these cultures in this fashion—there's terrible danger there! Be careful!"

Cal said nothing. The technicians grouped to the rear of Onia, looking intently towards the globe—then suddenly it suffused with a radiance and the swarming mist became alive, swirling with vast activity.

"It works!" Cal cried hoarsely, and tried to move out of his chair; but he was fixed there rigidly, his muscles locked. So he shouted: "Laj! Flenj! Quickly! Put the cultures in that bowl so they can escape. They're useless if imprisoned. Switch off that magnetizer!"

Laj was too leaden to obey, hardly able to stand on his feet—but Flenj moved swiftly enough. He unscrewed the top of the globe and tipped its contents into a large, shining bowl on the bench. Then he stood watching the swarming life surging within it.

"Yes, we've done it!" Cal breathed, watching fixedly.

Laj retreated hastily to his former position. Onia kept her eyes fixed on the cultures.

"They're alive, certainly," she agreed, "but you told them to attack plasma and stone, Cal. Suppose they attack us? We are rapidly passing into a stony mutation. That thought never occurred to me before, or perhaps to you." Her voice rose to a pitch which showed she was hardly capable of controlling her emotions any longer. "Cal, you shouldn't have done it! It means doom! Horrible doom. Why did you...?"

She made to stride forward towards him as he sat with his hands on the reflector switches, unable to turn his head to look at her. In fact he had not even heard her. The mutation of the weird coagulation in his blood stream was complete. He sat as a greying statue, completely motionless.

Onia took three strides towards him, her arm outflung to reach him—then she too stopped, every sense crushed into extinction, her eyes fixed on him.

The technicians looked at one another—but only Flenj and his comrade were still alive. Laj and Tilan were as immovable as Onia and Cal. Slowly the two remaining technicians moved back from the cultures swarming in the bowl on the bench. They procreated at lightning speed, moving in a packed mass up one side of the bowl until their very weight overbalanced it.

It dropped to the floor with a ringing clang, stopping when it came to within a few feet of Cal. The released cultures surged along the floor, up the bench, to the walls, growing—growing—growing into an ever-deepening tide....

CHAPTER NINE

Mona Driscoll's voice ceased speaking. She rubbed her forehead and then dragged her gaze away from blazing Sirius with a superhuman effort.

"That's...all I can remember," she whispered, and sat down on the nearest stony machine.

"Three hours you've been talking," Bob breathed, staring at her in amazement.

"Three hours? I wouldn't know. I was in a sort of trance. Don't ask me why I should have all that information, either. Maybe it's reincarnation, or something. Memory down the ages, and all that sort of thing.... Damned spooky, anyway!"

"Spooky nothing!" Bob cried. "Holy cats, no! I begin to get the hang of this business at last!"

"Congratulations, Mr. Holmes. Have a shot of cocaine."

"It fits in," Bob continued earnestly. "Don't you realize that these cultures with the tiny brains—brains nonetheless quite intelligent—would absorb far more knowledge than just the order to kill plasma and stone? That would be the basic order—just as our basic order of life is to eat and drink. That is a mechanical necessity; whatever else the cultures knew, they gleaned from actual observation. The cultures saw everything which happened in this laboratory, and knew perfectly well what was transpiring even before they were brought to actual animated life."

"Seems like that," Mona agreed, her brow wrinkled.

"They ate their way out of prison, procreating as they went—leaving the stony human beings alone. I don't know why, but possibly because calcified human tissue was not their kind of nourishment. As time went on they naturally handed on their mental impressions to their offspring. Myriads of the things spawned in the soil and found their way to the outer world. At that time, no doubt, the man of today was little better than a troglodyte; the people in this hall must have belonged to some super-race from a distant planet near Aldebaran...."

"Our primitive men would be bound to absorb some of the cultures into their systems, either with food or water. The intelligent activity of the cultures within them would affect their dull, stupid brains, giving rise to superstition, fear, and all the things which we today inherit."

"Uh-huh," Mona acknowledged, brooding.

"With the inexorable law of evolution," Bob went on, "the cultures would evolve into new species. Today we have thousands of invisible life forms, right up to visible insect life—and nearly all these forms of life attack and destroy stone! Science agrees that the erosion of stone is not so much caused by climatic conditions as by invisible life. To these evolved cultures there is no difference between real stone and the pseudo-stone life from the Companion of Sirius.... And incidentally, even the names of those two stars have been handed down, though the scientists who invented them probably imagined they were original."

"None of this explains why I, of all women, should turn into a walking history book!" Mona protested.

"But it does! Here and there some of the original cultures must be surviving—not dead, but dormant. Some cultures, diatoms, and suchlike stay that way for generations. Somewhere you must have picked up an original culture...."

"Now wait a minute...."

"I tell you, you picked up a culture!" Bob insisted. "Maybe from a cut finger; in your food—any place. So must thousands of other people too—but only you, of all these potential thousands, ever saw Sirius at close enough quarters, through 'Tiny,' to have his radiations affect you!"

"Eh?" Mona looked startled.

"The radiations of Sirius, quite detectable through 'Tiny's' mirror, passed through your optic nerves and invisibly affected your brain. The culture within you responded to the radiation and came to life! Being obviously in a position near your brain, it got the full force of the radiation transmitted through your eyes. It came to life from an unguessably long sleep, and each time it moved, you keeled over because of the brain pressure."

Mona gave a nauseated gesture. "This is loathsome, Bob! Besides, it's impossible! You've seen Sirius, same as I have—so have all the observatory workers. How come that only I...."

"Because you are the only one who happened to pick up a culture in your travels. I repeat: the culture came to life. Its memory stream was close enough to your own brain cells for you to be affected. As it stirred, you became dizzy and also received faint memory impressions from the moment you studied Sirius for the first time that night. The memory lasted a while and then faded again: the culture was not fully awake, But deep down in you thereafter was a rooted decision to stop me making the same mistake as this young scientist once did—the mistake of drawing stuff from other worlds....

"By steering clear of watching Sirius, memory began to die and the culture only stirred slightly at intervals, overbalancing you. But when you came to look at Sirius again here, he woke up once more. This time he remained awake and the whole story was transmitted to you. Understand?"

"I—I suppose so. And it's still horrible.... To think that I have a—a something, an intelligent mite, embedded in my brain! It's ghastly!"

Bob smiled a little. "Why? We're full of living mites, all of us. If it comes to that, a thinking one is a stage higher up the scale."

"I don't see it that way! And look, what exactly led we two of all people to this place? Amazing coincidence, wasn't it?"

"Maybe; maybe not." Bob mused over it. "It is said that history repeats itself. Perhaps we are only following a Time-circle back to the same place. It is even possible that I was once Cal—since my projector is identical to the one he made; and that you were once Onia, a fact explained by your uncanny knowledge of past events, not altogether attributable to that culture's assistance.... That's dead and finished, though, Right now we're Mr. and Mrs. Robert Driscoll, and I'm thinking about the world earthquakes. What we have here explains quite a lot."

"It does? I must have missed something."

"I didn't. Consider: once beyond the valley outside— beyond its floor, that is—this stone substance finishes. But it must have gone on propagating somewhere because, presumably, the cultures were not altogether successful in destroying it. Why, then, should it not travel below the surface of the Earth? After all, it was from the Companion of Sirius, therefore it seems that its one aim would be to get to a place where there is tons of pressure. Stuff from the Companion of Sirius holds the record for density and weight, remember. It exists under terrific compression. Where better to go than down into the Earth into ever-increasing density?"

"You may have something there," Mona agreed. "It's possible it has been going down for thousands of years—that it is responsible for earthquakes?"

"Why not?" Bob spread his hands. "Earthquakes are caused by inner displacement, but no scientist knows why the displacement occurs, because he has never been down to see! He can only assume.... I believe this stuff has been going down constantly, multiplying like a cancer, changing to hard stone as the pressure increases and so blocking up the natural hot outflows from volcanoes, earth's only safety-valves. Right now the blockages are serious. Half the volcanoes are working and half are not; if that doesn't point to blockage at the roots, what does? Something has got to blow up, or else! Hence the earthquakes. And right here is the beginning of the cancer which is causing all the trouble...."

Mona gave a despondent sigh. "We know all this and can't do a thing about it, Bob. Locked down here with no means of escape, and the world shaking harder every darned minute...!" She reflected and then resumed: "Of course, since all the cultures were knocked out of that bowl, some of them might never have come to life. If we could find them, get them started with Sirius radiation...."

"Hopeless!" Bob snorted. "It would take thousands of years for enough cultures to breed to destroy all the stone there now is in the world. There's got to be some other way, but I'm hanged if I know what."

"Well, I know when *I'm* licked." Mona got to her feet. "Just the same, I'd rather die on a full stomach. I'll go and grab some food from the plane wreck."

She went off and returned to find Bob still pacing around. The light of his torch was wavering now. Noting it, Mona put the canned concentrates down and prowled round inquisitively, finally discovering a stone switch on the wall. She depressed it and light gushed up instantly, intense blue-white light which had no shadows and which was presumably drawn from the solar storage batteries.

"There you are!" she exclaimed. Maybe you'll think better with a light on."

"An idea's buzzing around," Bob said absently, sitting down with concentrate on his knee. "It's crazy, fantastic—yet I don't see anything wrong with it."

"That's no criterion. Let's have it."

"Right! In the past centuries, the Companion of Sirius was a white dwarf of vastly heavy gas-life which, brought here, evolved and then turned into pseudo-stone."

"According to my memories, yes. A globe of gas-life."

"It was young then," Bob mused; "must have been because Sirius was young, too. But now the Companion of Sirius is mature, even as Earth is. So something must have happened on the Companion of Sirius which killed all the former gas-life, because today the Companion of Sirius is a part-solid, part-gaseous dwarf possessing material with a density two thousand times greater than platinum."

"Stop me if I'm wrong," Mona said, "but I do believe you are suggesting that there exists on the Companion of Sirius today a type of life which kills this other stone life."

"There must be, else what changed the other life but

a newer, higher form of life born out of the natural course of evolution? Just as new forms superseded our prehistoric juggernauts."

Mona relaxed. "And the condemned men ate a hearty breakfast!" she exclaimed. "We are here and you are light-years out in space! What good is all this to us while we're seated on kegs of dynamite?"

"Use what's left of your brain, sweetheart! There is a projector over there and I know how to work it. If I can reach the Companion of Sirius with it...."

"Maybe you've forgotten how far away Sirius is? Nearly eight light years!"

"And at the speed of light...." Bob frowned. "Mmm—that would mean four hundred and forty-three weeks—sixteen years. That was the problem Cal was up against and solved it. You can't remember what was in the formula Linida gave him, I suppose?"

"Afraid not...." Mona got to her feet. "Well, things being as they are, I'm going to look for some sort of radio equipment. Should be some somewhere here, according to my memory. I don't fancy passing out in the Hall of Fame even if you do. Maybe we can contact the outer world somehow."

She wandered away up the hall—then she suddenly stopped and Bob saw that she was swaying dizzily. He caught up with her and put a steadying arm about her shoulders.

"Old Man Culture on the move again, I guess," she said uncertainly. "Wish he'd stop shifting about; it gives me the devil of a headache...." Suddenly she gripped Bob's arm tightly. "Wait a minute! Some new sort of memory I'm getting...!"

She stopped talking, steadied herself, then walked in the fashion of a somnambulist to a machine near the reflector and projector. It was stone-covered, but even so it did not require a genius to see it was a giant mathematical computer.

"You'd—you'd better look this over'," Mona said, then she sat down heavily, a hand to her forehead. "Something led me to show it to you. Don't ask me why...."

Bob turned from her and studied the machine carefully. It was intricate beyond imagining, but at least the numerals made sense. Though they were not normal symbols, he could calculate from the positions where the units, tens, and hundreds came. After nearly twenty minutes of close scrutiny he swung around.

"I've just figured out what it is!" he cried. "It's a speed calculator of space distances, obviously for use with projector and telescope. But there's a set of figures here—the last set ever made apparently—which estimates that the distance to the region of Sirius can be covered in six hours there and back. That ties up with what Cal got from Linida, doesn't it?"

"Ties up exactly."

"Good! I think I know something about Old Man Culture too. You can receive his thoughts, therefore he can no doubt receive yours. He realized what was going on between you and me—that we were stymied. His one aim in life is to destroy stone. He had the chance to know from his earlier existence what the scientists did, and so he passed the information on to us—a friend, Mona, a rare, queer friend!"

"Queer is right," Mona said, shuddering.

Bob was not listening to her. He turned to the projector and spent an hour or more inspecting the controls.

"Four-dimensional processes all right," he proclaimed at length. "The basic operation of remote control is the same as my own, but these guys managed to foreshorten space. Too complicated to work out here. Seems to me that if I use this thing as I would have done on my own, it will work. No harm in trying. Just a matter of gearing it to strike the Companion of Sirius."

This he found a fairly difficult task—but not impossible. It amounted to a variation of figures on the computer, and the depression of a switch—then the stone-freed tubes on the giant apparatus began to glow brightly.

"If this works," he said, "we'll have a piece of Companion of Sirius material here within six hours. All we can do is sit around and wait."

"It'll be an improvement on sixteen years, anyway," Mona commented dryly. "I'm going to have another look for the radio."

"May as well help you," Bob said, and they began to walk about, investigating together.

"There's something I don't quite understand," Mona said presently. "If we do get something from the

Companion, how is it going to pass through this rock roof? Matter won't go through matter."

"Didn't I say the fourth dimension? This device operates through that. In the fourth dimension matter is wide open."

Mona was not listening. She hurried forward suddenly to an instrument and then gave a sigh of disappointment.

"This was a radio apparatus," she said, with a rueful glance. "Seems part of the roof fell in and cracked it up.... I've an awfully uncomfortably feeling, Bob, that we're locked in more tightly than we ever imagined. It's hard to realize all at once that we may never get out."

"There don't seem to be any explosives around, either. Of course, there is a chance that the stuff from the Companion may start eating a way out for us."

Mona nodded, none too hopefully. "In the meantime, we have six hours to kill. I'm going to grab some shut-eye."

She relaxed on a long, stony machine and soon began to doze. She was awakened again by Bob shaking her violently.

"Mona, wake up! It's come! What's more, it works!"

"Eh? Who works what...? Oh!" She blinked into wakefulness. "The—the stuff you mean...?"

"Sure! Take a look at this!"

Bob caught her arm eagerly and whirled her to the projector. She stood gazing at a lump of irregular grey substance on the transmission-plate.

"Life substance from the Companion," Bob explained. "It's incredibly heavy. I have to use this electric cutter to hack pieces off. A piece about half an inch square weighs about a hundredweight." Bob paused. then added: "On Earth most of our solid forms, like cliffs and things, are actually built up of life forms of minute size. Evidently the same thing happens on the Companion of Sirius—but this definitely puts paid to the primitive stone type of life. Watch!"

He picked up a fragment, literally staggered with it across the laboratory, then dropped it with a thud on the nearest stone section. Immediately there began a curious faint hissing noise, accompanied by the gradual diminishment of the stone and a widening of the grey-white substance.

"Get it?" Bob questioned eagerly.

Mona frowned. "Not quite. It looks as though we've exchanged one trouble for another. This stuff grows by consuming the other...."

"Naturally! Lower forms of life always increase by consuming still lower ones. But we can replace stone by this other substance. And it is pliable, not rigid. It will not seal things up as the stone has done. Once it has destroyed the stone existing deep down in the earth, it will free the normal volcanic channels."

"Won't take long either," Mona said. "It's spreading fast."

"Uh-huh—multiplying all the while. The more stone it consumes and breaks down into its own life-form, the larger it will get—Mona, I've got it! All we need are as many masses of this stuff as possible from the Companion, and we're all set. They can be distributed to the danger areas—mainly over volcano bases. Inside a week the blocked channels will be freed...."

"Maybe you're forgetting we're still in here?"

"Not for long we won't be. This stuff will eat a way to the open in double quick time."

Bob gathered up some more of the material and blundered with it into the narrow little space beyond the hall. Fizzing noises came forth. Coming back he said:

"One projector like this won't be enough. We'll need some more resembling it...."

He broke off, startled by a growling rumble deep under the laboratory. It increased to a tremendous vibration, roaring in from all sides.

"Earthquake!" Mona cried hoarsely. "Another one! Quick! We stand a better chance in our original cubby hole. Any of these things might fall on top of us...."

But even as she turned and fled for the gap in the wall the earthquake broke—in all its fury. The floor shook violently, flinging Bob from his feet and sending Mona reeling forward.

Rock began to rain inwards from the roof. From where he scrambled to his feet again, Bob gazed in speechless dismay as a mighty length of stone came crashing down in the midst of the projector, smashing it into a thousand pieces. Then the view was hidden in blinding dust.

"This is the end of...," Mona started to shout; then

she stopped as a chunk of rock sailed towards her. It struck her on the forehead, sending her toppling backwards through the fissure into the cavity beyond.

Bob swung round. The lights went out at that moment as stone rained down on the solar generators. He jerked out his dim torch and floundered through dust and ruin into the small space beyond.

The substance from the Companion was still hissing and spluttering around and overhead. Deep down, the rumbles of the latest earth-spasm were dying away... but the damage was done now. The hall of science was buried and smashed forever.

"Mona!" Bob cried, scrambling to her. Mona...!"

His torch beam showed that her forehead was bleeding badly. She stirred weakly in his grip as he pressed a handkerchief to the wound.

"Mona—wake up! That's it—! Only a flesh wound. You'll be O.K."

"Are we still in the hall?" she whispered.

"No, it's smashed. Everything is. Projector gone—and with it our last hope of saving this exploding world. Only ourselves to try and save now, I guess. We've got to...."

"Listen, Bob—listen!" She caught his arm tightly. "You have a pencil and notebook?"

"Sure. But what...."

"Take this down!"

She was apparently only half-conscious, but Bob scribbled busily as she talked. Her voice was a steady monotone as though she were repeating something out of a book. The more he wrote, the more astounded Bob became.

"Say!" he interrupted her. "You're describing a complete four-dimensional projector! How on earth...."

"Write!" she commanded. "Time's precious!"

Again he went on. Ten minutes—twenty minutes. When at last Mona had stopped, he scratched his head dazedly over that which he had taken down.

"A four-dimensional projector, a means by which my own projector can be made four-dimensional! Mona, how did you...?"

She moved as he caught her in his arms again. Her voice became normal once more.

"Did you get it?" she asked.

"Yes, I got it.... " He dabbed at her bleeding forehead. "Do you know what you said...?"

"Not now I don't; not clearly, anyway. All I did was repeat the thoughts I received. Old Man Culture again. It seems that this crack I got on the skull nearly put paid to him. He realized from my thoughts that we had lost everything, but he knew all about the projector and gave me the details before he passed out. This forehead cut must have struck right at him— Maybe he's been washed away with the blood I've lost. Anyway, he's dead. And so, I hope, are my dizzy spells."

Bob stared at her in the flickering torchlight.

"Do you begin to understand what this means?" he asked.

"Of course I do! You can use your projector after all, and give it a four-dimensional setup. Then you can get stuff from the Companion of Sirius and have the scientists go to work repairing this old globe of ours. It will vindicate you at the observatory, Bob. You can do the job in time; you'll have to!"

"I will!" he muttered. "It means much more than that too. I'll be made a master-scientist. It will be the dawn of a new age of science in which old laws are remade in the light of four-dimensional knowledge. Then...."

He glanced up sharply at a sudden cracking and the feel of water dripping in his face.

"The opening!" he cried. "That stuff has gotten through!"

He lifted Mona to her feet, supporting her as she climbed unsteadily up the rocky, spluttering cavity side to the top. At last they had scrambled out together into a grey dawn filled with lowering rainclouds.

The plane was still there, as they had left it.

"We made it!" Bob exclaimed, patting his notebook in his jacket pocket. "If only those frozen unknowns back there knew what they had done for us! They didn't save their own generation, but they did save ours!"

"Maybe they do know," Mona said quietly. "Didn't you say yourself that Time is a circle? Come on—I can hardly wait until the President starts pinning medals on your manly chest. Besides, it's wet out here!"

ABOUT THE AUTHOR

British writer **JOHN RUSSELL FEARN** was born near Manchester, England, in 1908. As a child he devoured the science fiction of Wells and Verne, and was a voracious reader of the Boys' Story Papers. He was also fascinated by the cinema, and first broke into print in 1931 with a series of articles in *Film Weekly*.

He then quickly sold his first novel, *The Intelligence Gigantic*, to the American magazine, *Amazing Stories*. Over the next fifteen years, writing under several pseudonyms, Fearn became one of the most prolific contributors to all of the leading US science fiction pulps, including such legendary publications as *Astounding Stories*, *Startling Stories*, *Thrilling Wonder Stories*, and *Weird Tales*.

During the late 1940s he diversified into writing novels for the UK market, and also created his famous superwoman character, The Golden Amazon, for the prestigious Canadian magazine, the Toronto *Star Weekly*. In the early 1950s in the UK, his fifty-two novels as "Vargo Statten" were bestsellers, most notably his novelization of the film, *Creature from the Black Lagoon*.

Apart from science fiction, he had equal success with westerns, romances, and detective fiction, writing an amazing total of 180 novels—most of them in a period of just ten years—before his early death in 1960. His work has been translated into nine languages, and continues to be reprinted and read worldwide.

www.ingramcontent.com/pod-product-compliance
Lightning Source LLC
Chambersburg PA
CBHW022152260626
47155CB00017B/1850